ON THE
DEVIL'S COURT

ON THE DEVIL'S COURT

Carl Deuker

LITTLE, BROWN AND COMPANY
Boston   Toronto   London

To Anne Mitchell

The author wishes to thank the editor of this novel, Ms. Ann Rider, for her sound advice and needed encouragement.

Library of Congress Cataloging-in-Publication Data
Deuker, Carl.
    On the Devil's court. / Carl Deuker. — 1st ed.
        p.   cm.
    Summary: Struggling with his feelings of inadequacy and his failure to make the basketball team in his new school, seventeen-year-old Joe Faust finds himself willing to trade his soul for one perfect season of basketball.
    ISBN 0-316-18147-1
    [1. Basketball — Fiction.   2. Self-acceptance — Fiction.]
I. Title.
PZ7.D4930n.1988
[Fic] — dc19   88-13432
                                                                              CIP
                                                                               AC

Joy Street Books are published by Little, Brown and Company (Inc.)

10   9   8   7   6   5   4   3   2

FG

Published simultaneously in Canada
by Little, Brown & Company (Canada) Limited

PRINTED IN THE UNITED STATES OF AMERICA

PART
ONE

1

There are two things that I'm ashamed of. The first is that I agreed to sell my soul to the devil. But I'll go into that later. The second is that I've always gone to a private school. My father makes me. He went to a private school. My mother went to a private school. They met at a private-school dance.

Back East it wasn't so bad. In Boston all the kids — or at least all the kids on my block — went to private schools. Then my father, the great Professor Joseph Faust, Sr., came home from Harvard one day and announced he had accepted the position of Chairman of the Department of Genetics at the University of Washington. My father is one of those scientists who recombine genes so that monkeys turn into marigolds, or something like that. Anyway, the job meant more money and more prestige for him, so off we went.

I didn't want to leave, even though my life wasn't exactly perfect in Boston. My dad and I haven't seen eye to eye for as long as I can remember. The problem is he's great at almost everything. I have to sweat for B's; he breezed to straight A's from the cradle through Stanford grad school. I wet my bed until I was eight; I bet he never even wore diapers. He doesn't understand a son who isn't perfect like he is. His whole life is one long, boring tale of fame and fortune. My whole life is one short, boring story of mediocrity.

It isn't easy having a great man for a father. We'll be eating a burger at McDonald's and some jerk will thrust his hand between the french fries and the milk shake and bellow, "Oh, Dr. Faust, sorry to bother you. I'm Joe Idiot and I saw you on TV and I think what you do is great." Or we'll be at some high-class play and during intermission some sixty-year-old hippo with a diamond necklace bouncing on her crinkly cleavage will waddle up and croon, "Dr. Faust, you don't know me, but I'm Mrs. Moron and I just had to tell you that I think it will be a crime if you don't win the Nobel Prize."

His is a tough act to follow. Other kids shoplift, get drunk, throw chairs through school windows. If I get a C+ on my report card you'd think I murdered a nun. His face grows ten feet long; his eyebrows furrow; his voice drops to a deep baritone. "Joseph, Stanford doesn't take C plus students."

I'd be happier if he were at least a klutz like most brainy types, an Elmer Fudd who lives in the library and looks like one of those white worms that squirm around under rotting logs in the forest.

Not my dad. I've grown recently and have put on a few pounds, but I'm basically a gangly redhead with more than a few zits. My dad is tall, permanently tan, and built like a truck. He smokes two packs a day but makes up for it by working out four times a week at the faculty gym. Hand him a football and he'll whip a thirty-yard spiral on a line. Put a bat in his hand and he'll pound a baseball right out of the park.

But my dad has one weak spot. He can't play basketball. He stares at the ball when he dribbles, so he's always bouncing it off his feet. He crosses his legs on defense, so it's simple to take the baseline on him. And he can't shoot; he throws up brick after brick. I've explained to him how to dribble; I've demonstrated how to play defense; I've shown him how to shoot. He never listens to me. On my thirteenth birthday I beat him for the first time. Within two months I wasn't just beating him, I was annihilating him. He lost so many games in our driveway that he did what he tells me never to do. He quit. He won't play against me anymore. In Boston he even found excuses to stay away from my games.

He'd wish me luck as I headed out the door. "I'm

on the verge of something, Joe," he'd say. "I've just got to work tonight. You understand, don't you?"

I understood all right.

2

My parents thought I was stupid to choose the attic room in our new house. They warned me it would be a sweatbox in the summer and mold city in the winter. I told them I loved the view. My bedroom was perched on the top of an old three-story home in the Sunset Hill neighborhood. And there were huge windows facing in three directions. To the southeast was snowy Mount Rainier; the jagged Cascade Range was to the east; and to the west was Puget Sound, which was backed — on clear days — by the Olympic Mountains.

But that was the problem: it's never clear in Seattle. It was raining on June 15 when we moved in and it was still raining a week later when the boxes were finally empty and summer officially began. So it wasn't because of the view that I chose that room. Things just seem to go better when my mother has a little extra space to herself.

Most people have a definite picture of what a professor's wife should look like. They're supposed to be well-groomed and well-dressed, but a little gray and slightly overweight. They spend their days lifting lids off simmering saucepans and their nights playing bridge with "the girls."

My mother isn't like that at all.

To begin with, she looks like a starlet. She has deep red hair and dark brown eyes. As for her figure, my father used to say that she was big in all the right places. He doesn't say that anymore — because he knows I'm old enough to know what he means — but it's still true.

Not that she's the dumb-broad type — not by a long shot. She's an artist, a successful sculptress who's pretty famous in the art world under her maiden name, Ella Frank. Put a piece of clay in her hands and it turns into a small bear or a tiny kangaroo. She doesn't keep these little masterpieces. She just wads them up and slaps them back into the mound of clay they came from. They don't matter to her; she can always do another one. Besides, her specialty isn't sculptures of animals, or trees, or famous people. I wish it were. For the last eight years her specialty has been sculptures of men — naked men.

She should have told me about it in the beginning, though I guess it would have been tough for her. Still, that first discovery was plenty tough for me.

I was in the fourth grade and had just gotten a blue star on my arithmetic test. Miss Sangster (we called her "the gangster") didn't give out many stars. All day I had that paper on top of my binder so that the other kids would see it and know how smart

I was. When the final bell rang, I ran straight home, shot up the stairs to my mother's studio, and for the first and last time rushed in without knocking.

"Look! Mother! Look!" I shouted. But it wasn't mother I was talking to. It was him. He was standing there, naked and hairy, next to the fern. I turned around and shot back down the stairs.

My mother came down right after me. I don't remember a word of her explanation, but when she was done she lit one of those little black cigarettes she smoked before she quit and said, "You're not upset anymore, are you?"

I shook my head.

"Good. Now what did you want to show me?"

My arithmetic paper was all crumpled up in my fist, and the blue star had fallen off. We smoothed the paper out on the kitchen table and she kissed me on the forehead and told me how proud she was of me. Then she helped me look for the blue star, but we never did find it.

My mother's work hasn't bothered me for a while. Art is art, after all. And now that I'm older I can appreciate the beauty of what she does. But I'll admit I don't enjoy bumping into the latest Mr. Muscle, so having the top floor entirely to myself was worth damp armpits and mildew on the wall.

I spent two days painting. I chose cobalt blue for the walls and pale blue for the trim and the doors. I put my John Lennon poster next to the window looking out over the Sound because it seemed right that it should be there. Then I stuck some pictures from *Sports Illustrated*'s swimsuit issue on the inside of my closet door. Lots of guys my age have centerfolds on their walls, but my mother would never go for that. Finally, I put my Magic Johnson poster on the ceiling over the bed.

I'm a Celtics fan, but there's no denying that Magic is the greatest ever. You just see him lead the fast break once and you know it. His hands flick out and knock the ball loose. He pounces on it and those long legs propel him down the court toward the hoop. He looks left, fakes right, and then dishes back to the left. It's a pass your old lady could handle, right where you want it, right when you want it. Two points.

But Magic can do more than lead a fast break. Post him up and he's almost as tough as McHale. Clear out a side and he can take it to the hole like Michael Jordan. Those days I thought I'd give anything to be able to play like Magic.

After I put his poster up, I spent the next week lying on my back staring up at it. If it sounds boring, imagine doing it. The fact is I was lonely. I never thought much of the guys in Boston when I was there. Ron Moody was nothing more than a goon and Konray had the heart of a murderer. They both were lucky to have rich parents who could keep them out of juvenile hall. But Brindle and Steve Dowell both played one-on-one fair and square.

And afterward they were always good for a soda and some video games at Dobeson's Grocery. There were other guys too, guys who I knew and who just sort of knew me. Nobody knew me in Seattle, so I hung around my room, listening to music and looking out those big windows.

I noticed the school first thing. It was about two blocks away and guys played basketball there almost every morning. Part of me felt like going down and seeing if I could get in with them. But part of me was just too lazy, or scared to make the effort.

That first week my mother and father were so busy unpacking and arguing that they didn't notice I wasn't going out. They'd ask me at breakfast how I'd slept and I'd say, "Fine." They'd ask at lunch how my unpacking was going and I'd mumble, "OK." They'd ask at dinner how my day had been and I'd get by with "Not bad."

It couldn't last. As soon as they got done putting up their art prints they got their fingerprints all over me. "Joe, have you met any of the boys in the neighborhood?" . . . "Joe, why don't you see if you can still get on a summer league baseball team?" . . . "Joe, don't you think you should at least go outside?"

3

I hit the streets on a Monday morning. It was gray, as usual. I had on my Celtics T-shirt, cutoffs, and my high-top Converse basketball shoes. I ate a quick breakfast and headed to the playground.

I liked Loyal High right from the start. It was an old wooden box of a school, but the paint job was something else. The wood siding was an ordinary beige, but the trim was done in purple and deep red. It gave the place an enchanted feeling, like a school in a fairy tale. And I liked the name. I wasn't sure where it came from or what it was supposed to mean, but the idea of being loyal appealed to me.

The three basketball courts were off to the side, and only the center court had nets at both ends. That was the court where the pickup games were played. I stayed off it. There's nothing to be gained by being pushy.

I shot around on a side court that had a bent rim and a ripped red, white, and blue net. There was nobody else in sight, but it was early, not even nine-thirty. I warmed up and waited.

I've always been able to shoot well. The ball just feels good in my hands. Actually, it's not in the hands but in the fingertips where the feel is. If I get the ball up in my fingertips, and if I follow through with my wrist, the ball is going in. There is absolutely nothing like the sound of a perfect swish.

Being able to shoot made me a starter, even as a freshman, at Emerson. That's because it was a small, private school and we only played against other small, private schools.

Let's face it, lots of kids in private schools know the etymology of *aardvark,* but they don't know what a backdoor play is. They can spell *dribble* in their cribs, but they can't do it at sixteen. Even the guys on my team at Emerson weren't really players, not like the kids in the big public schools, not like I wanted to be. My teammates would hustle out of the gym at the end of practice so they could get to the library to do some extra-credit assignment. But I kept shooting. I wore out the hoop in practice and I wore it out on game day, too.

Those days of small schools and soft competition were over. My father had all but promised I could go to a public school in Seattle. It was his way of softening the blow of our move. And I knew the minute I saw Loyal High that it was the place for me. That meant I'd be playing in the Metro League. I'd be a new senior trying out against fifteen guys the coach already knew. I'd been a big fish in a little pond in Boston. In Seattle I was a minnow about to be dropped into the ocean, and I wasn't sure I'd be able to swim. But I was ready to try.

When the other guys finally came that first day, they came in two groups. The first four came up 24th Avenue. I figured they lived in Ballard, a Scandinavian neighborhood full of small, older houses. The other four came the same way I had — from 80th Street. That meant they probably lived near me on Sunset Hill where the homes were larger and had views of the Sound.

While they warmed up there was lots of laughter and kidding around. There were also eight of them — even teams. No one so much as nodded in my direction.

I didn't want to just stand and watch, and I didn't want to go home, so I went into my practice routine while they played. I put up twenty jumpers off the right-hand dribble; then twenty off the left. I did ten driving lay-ins from the right, ten from the left, ten right up the gut. I concentrated on my shots, but all the time I had one eye on the game going on next to me.

I wanted my chance.

4

Some of the guys were good, there was no denying it. But I didn't think any of them were out of my class. I stuck around because I had a feeling that someone would fall and cut up a knee or have to quit because Aunt Alice was visiting.

My hunch was right. In a scramble for a rebound a wild elbow caught this blond kid right in the eye. The eye instantly started to close up. There was nothing for him to do but go home and ice it. He was barely off the court when the call came.

"Hey, you want to play?"

It was a weird game. The matchups were pretty even except for one guy, Ross. He was the one who threw the elbow, and he was a super player. He was around six two, like me, had good hands, quick feet, and great timing. He dribbled like a guard and drove to the hoop like a forward. He even rebounded well. Ross was a high-school Magic Johnson. He scored the first ten points of the game, stole the ball twice, and rebounded all of my team's missed shots. He was so good that it was hard to keep playing. I just wanted to stop and watch.

Maybe that was the problem with his team. Maybe that's what his teammates were doing — watching. They should have buried us, but we hung in there. After ten minutes we were down 20–14; after twenty we had tied them at 36. Then our center, a stiff-legged but strong guy named John Lustik, hit two jump shots and I scored a couple of hoops off steals. At the end, Ross forced up some bad shots and we won, 50–46.

Afterward Ross came up and asked my name. "You play pretty good."

I shrugged. "We got a little lucky."

"You going to Loyal next year?"

I nodded.

Ross smiled. "Starting tomorrow you and me are going to play on the same team."

That afternoon the sun came out.

5

For the rest of that week I could hardly wait to get out of the house and onto the court. We played game after game, and I was always on Ross's team. I don't know how it happened, or why the other guys never said anything. All I know is that was how it was.

With Ross and me on the same team, it should have been no contest. We should have just piled up the victories. But for some reason we could never get into a good rhythm. If Ross drove the lane on a fast break, I'd never have a feel for whether he was going to keep it himself or dish it off. And when I drove around a screen he set, he never could sense whether to crash the boards or look for the pass off the pick-and-roll. Usually, after you play with someone for a while, especially someone you like, you pick up things like that. But with Ross it never came.

We didn't play smart either. We both tried to make great passes, to thread the needle when no one was expecting it. It worked if we were dishing off to one another. But if the miracle pass were going to one of the other guys, chances are it would hit him in the gut or go right through him and out of bounds. We'd glare at him and he'd clap his hands together like it could never happen again, but it did — over and over. Coach Anderson always said that a smart player knows the capabilities of his teammates. We played dumb.

Turnovers hurt, especially when the other team has a rock like John in the middle. "Deadly Dull" is what Ross called John, even to his face. John never let Ross get to him, though. He just went out and played every minute of every game the same: hard. He kept his hands up on defense; he blocked out on rebounds; he moved well without the ball. He shot when he was open, passed off when he was covered. Nothing flashy, just sound basketball. And most of the time his team won.

I don't like losing, but I can live with it, so long as I feel like I gave it my best and the other guy was just a little better. But that's not how it was.

After we'd lost some game we should have won, I'd squat down under the hoop and try to figure out how it had slipped away. Losing ate at me. But it didn't eat at Ross. Thirty seconds after the game was over he'd be at the water fountain sticking his finger over the spout and spraying the other guys. And his exuberance was contagious; it was impossible to stay away. So sooner or later I'd be over there with him fooling around, too.

6

On Saturday Ross didn't show and the games were lousy. He had kind of a fire he carried with him. If he liked you, if he let you inside the circle, you wanted to stay near. And if he froze you out, you wanted to make him pay for it. He was the most popular guy on the court — and the most hated. Everybody played harder when he was there.

But without him around, the guys drifted off early. After an hour or so John and I were the only ones left. We tried playing some one-on-one, but we didn't match up at all. John was too big for me inside, and I ate him alive outside. After a couple of games we gave it up.

"I wonder why Ross didn't show," I said as I pulled on my sweats.

"He caddies weekends at Broadmoor," John answered. "Or at least he did last summer."

"So he won't be here tomorrow, either?"

"Who knows? You can never tell with Ross. But I doubt it."

I went late the next day. I hadn't planned on going, but a lousy basketball game is better than no game at all. I was about half a block away when I heard Ross scream, "In your face! In your face!" I started walking faster.

When I reached the court, Ross stopped the game so that we could pick new teams and I could play. Some of the guys groaned, but Ross pushed until he got his way. For the next two hours we ran the court together. I'd feed him passes and he'd put up the most impossible, incredible shots. And when they went down, he'd give me a high-five or point his finger at me and chant: "You! You! You!"

I could have played all day, but some of the guys

had things they had to do. We dropped down to three-on-three, then two-on-two. Finally even John left. Ross and I shot for a few minutes, then he said he had to go. But as we were walking off the court he asked me if I could get a car that night.

"Yeah. Or at least I think so. Where do you want to go?"

"It's a surprise. I'll meet you right here around ten. OK?"

I couldn't ask for the car for no reason at all, so I had to lie and tell my parents I was going to the movies. And since nothing starts at ten o'clock, I had to leave the house at eight-thirty.

I drove down to the Peaches in Ballard Square and walked up and down the aisles looking at albums until I was sure they figured I was a shoplifter or a weirdo or both. It was still only nine-fifteen; Crown Books was closed so I couldn't go there and flip through *Penthouse*. I drove up to Loyal High, parked the car, and waited.

It was a little creepy sitting there in the dark. The minutes crawled by. At ten o'clock, I started looking around, but Ross didn't show. I put my head against the window and closed my eyes. The next thing I knew, Ross was pounding on the hood. I jumped up so fast I banged my head. "Let's go!" he said when I opened the door for him.

He still wouldn't tell me what was up. He just kept saying that I should relax and that it would be fun. He gave directions and I drove. I didn't like it much, but I did it. Once we crossed the Montlake Bridge I was completely lost. I'd never been in that part of the city before. He had me turn left at a store that made artificial arms and legs, and it wasn't until we were halfway down this wide avenue heading toward Lake Washington that he said anything at all.

"I got fired today."

"How come?"

"I sat on a white bench."

"What?"

"Caddies are supposed to sit on these old beat-up green benches. I sat on a white one, some old duffer complained, and they fired me."

Ross leaned forward and pointed to a side street. "Pull in there," he said. "Park the car and kill the lights."

We sat for about five minutes, then he opened the door and softly closed it. When the dome light went on, I noticed that he had a brown bag with him.

We walked along on the side street for about fifty yards, and then Ross ducked in behind some bushes. I followed him. He hoisted himself up and over a brick wall, and I tumbled after him.

"Shhh!" he said when I landed in a stack of leaves.

I could tell we were on a golf course from the sand traps in the moonlight. Ross looked around for a second and then motioned for me to follow him as he ran across the fairway. It was so dark that when he disappeared into the bushes on the other side, I lost him completely. I stood out in the fairway until I heard him call my name. "Stay close!" he said when I finally caught up with him.

We walked up a grassy knoll and then down to a creek. When we reached a bridge, Ross took two cans of spray paint out of the bag. "Here," he said as he handed one to me. "Go to work!"

"No way. I'm not writing anything."

He glared at me for a second. "All right, but keep a lookout."

Ross knelt down and started spraying obscenities on the boards of the bridge. The only sound was the wind in the trees and the hissing of the spray can.

I'd never been with anyone who'd done anything like that before. I should have walked away. I had the car; Ross would have had to follow. But I didn't move. I just watched him, and I kept thinking how astonished my father would be if he ever found out. I was scared, but it was exciting. And I felt strangely powerful, as if I were capable of things I hadn't dreamed of.

Ross finished spraying and stood up.

"Let's get out of here!" I whispered.

"Not yet. We've got one more thing to do." Then he ran along the side of the fairway and headed up toward the brightly lit clubhouse. We stopped about a hundred yards from it.

"This is stupid," I said. "We're going to get caught."

Ross shook his head. "No, we won't." He pointed to a little shack. "See that? The night watchman sits in that room smoking cigarettes and watching porno videos. We've got nothing to worry about. Just keep quiet and follow me."

We ran right through the lights. If anybody was looking, they'd have seen us clear as day. It was the fastest hundred I've ever run in my life.

I kept my eye on the shack as Ross went to work on that beautiful white wall. He had written a few of the standard things when we heard the footsteps. Immediately he dropped the can and we took off.

"Hey! Stop! You hear me? Stop!"

We ran faster, across the fairway and into the bushes. Ross dropped to the ground and grabbed my leg and pulled me down right next to him. My heart was pounding. Then I saw the beam of the flashlight.

The watchman was on the other side of the fairway, about thirty yards away. I couldn't see him, but when his light hit a bush or a tree it blazed up like it was under a spotlight. "I know you're there," we heard him say. "I can wait. I'll get you. I'll get you if I have to wait until morning."

Then the light bobbed up and down in the darkness as he crossed the fairway and headed right toward us. I put my face right down into the dirt and felt Ross next to me doing the same thing. The watchman moved the light in a wide arc, and for a split second it was right over our heads. Then it was gone.

We lay perfectly still as he strode up and down the fairway pointing his flashlight into the bushes. Finally he gave up and slowly made his way up the hill toward the clubhouse.

"Let's go!" Ross whispered and he was off like a shot. I stumbled along after him as best I could. He knew the course, but I didn't, so he had to stop and wait for me. We ran across the bridge, through the trees, and then I fell into a sand trap. He pulled me out of that, and the next thing I knew we were at the brick wall and up and over. We should have walked to the car, but we ran the whole way. I got in, started it up, and floored it.

"Don't ever pull that again," I said when we were safely away. "Why didn't you tell me what the deal was?"

"Hey, I wanted to surprise you."

"No way, Ross. Don't ever do it again. Understand?"

"OK, OK. I'll tell you next time. No big deal."

We drove in silence. I was so mad I didn't say a single word.

But once we crossed the University Bridge I felt calmer, and by the time we hit Phinney Ridge my hands weren't shaking at all. When we reached

Market Street, Ross fished around in his back pocket for his wallet. "You hungry?"

"Yeah," I admitted. "I'm starving."

"Stop at Burger King. I'll buy you a Whopper."

By the time I finished my first burger I wasn't mad anymore, and as I ate my second one we were both laughing, thinking about how stupid we were to have hidden when we could have just kept running. That old guy never would have caught us.

7

I had friends. I had basketball. It was warm and summertime and it should have been smooth sailing. But it wasn't. Somehow it never is.

I still had to eat dinner at home, and that's when I had unpleasant conversations with my father. "You'll need to score around thirteen hundred to get into Stanford," he kept telling me. "But don't worry, you can do it."

In Boston I hadn't done well on the PSAT. "You had the flu that week," my father had said when the scores arrived in the mail. "You'll improve on the SAT."

I'd nodded and pretended to agree with him, but I'd felt fine the day of the PSAT. I didn't see how I could have done any better.

My father was all lathered up about college, but

I wasn't. It was still a year away. I was much more excited about my final year of high school. I was looking forward to lacing up my sneakers and laying it on the line against the best players in the city. And it wasn't just because of basketball that I was looking forward to public school. I'd seen the public school kids every day in Boston. They seemed freer than us, not just in the way they dressed, but in their whole lives. That's how Ross was; that's how I wanted to be.

I thought it was set, but out of the blue one July day my father started running on about this wonderful private school across Lake Washington in Bellevue. "Most of the professors send their children to Eastside Academy. It's quite a place. The kids really like it. Not stuffy like the private schools in Boston. I know how tired you are of that sort of thing. Eastside is different, casual. I'm sure you'd fit right in. And high grades from a place like Eastside count for a lot."

I did my best to ignore him, but my father is a hard person to ignore. By the end of the week he'd gotten hold of Eastside's recommended summer reading list, and the day after that I found a stack of books outside the door to my room with a little note on top: "These look interesting to me!"

It took two trips to carry them into my room and dump them in the back of my closet. I didn't pay attention to any of the books except the one on top — *The Tragical History of the Life and Death of Doctor Faustus*. When you see something that's got your name on the cover, it's hard not to be a little interested.

Monday night I shot pool with Ross, and when I hit the sack I couldn't sleep. So I flicked on the light and grubbed around in the closet until I found that book. I vaguely remember my mother telling me the story when I was little. It's about a guy who sells his soul to the devil. I sort of hoped the book would be interesting, but it turned out to be one of those old plays full of *thee*'s and *thou*'s. It looked like slow going, but I did flip through and look at the pictures. The best one was on the title page. It showed an old guy with a full beard and a pointy mustache. He had a book in one hand and a curved staff in the other. He was wearing long, flowing robes and one of those caps you put on for graduation. He stood inside a charmed circle formed by all these weird symbols. At the man's feet, kneeling down just outside the magic circle, was this gruesome devil with long, thin fingers and horns like a ram. His skin was leathery and spiky things came right out of it. He was an ugly-looking devil, but the man didn't seem frightened. He looked like he had things under control.

I didn't put the book away. Instead, I opened it to page seven and laid it on top of my desk. If I flipped a couple pages over every day, my father would think I was doing something constructive with my time, as he'd have put it. There would be one less thing to fight about.

8

I can't say we fought about Ross, but it would have been better if I'd never mentioned him. Once I did, my parents were all over me to meet him. "Bring him around for lunch some Saturday," my mother said. "He sounds like quite a guy," my father added.

It seemed like a simple request, but I knew they wouldn't like Ross. He wouldn't go through the "Yes, sir . . . no, ma'am" routine that snowed them every time. There was always a mocking laugh in Ross's eyes. I was afraid my mother and father would think that Ross was laughing at them.

After the first couple weeks, I stopped mentioning him around the house. But my parents weren't stupid. They knew I played basketball with him every morning and fooled around the city with him at night. They also knew something wasn't quite right, and they weren't happy about it.

They've always been on me about friends, maybe because they feel guilty that I'm an only child. They worry that I don't have enough friends, or that my friends are the wrong type — that sort of thing. In Boston my father used to force guys on me.

There was one kid, Chucky, who was the nightmare of my life before we moved. He was fat and smart and he wore funny light blue slacks and dark gold shirts. His father, Dr. Striebing, was my father's racquetball partner. While they were whacking the ball off the walls of the Lexington Racquet Club, I was whacking Chucky all over the backyard. He must have hated me as much as I hated him.

Every time Chucky was supposed to come over I'd complain. I'd tell my dad that I wished Chucky would die so that I could see him stretched out in a blue and gold coffin. But Chucky came from a good family; therefore Chucky was a good friend. That was my father's logic and there was no changing him. So at barbecues and baseball games it was me and Chucky, over and over.

My dad probably wished he could bring Chucky along to Seattle. But he couldn't, so when August rolled around and my parents still hadn't met any of my new friends, my dad decided to take action.

We were eating dinner on a Friday night. My father mentioned that he was having a research partner and his wife over on Sunday. It was no big deal, he often had people over. I grunted and shoveled in more mashed potatoes. Then it came. "By the way," he added, "you'll be glad to hear that my colleague lives right in the neighborhood and has a son who happens to be your age."

I almost choked. I could just imagine this son: glasses and calculators, the debate team and the chess club. Chucky all over again. I wished Sunday would never come.

But it did, right after Saturday. I spent the afternoon looking out the window and listening to Bruce Springsteen. It was a clear day and, for Seattle, hot. My mother was right about my room, though I didn't admit it to her. The windows turned it into a sweatbox. If I wanted a Coke I had to climb down all those stairs. If I drank it in the kitchen, I'd be thirsty by the time I made it back to my room. But if I carried the Coke upstairs, I'd slop half of it on the carpet. So I just stayed put and waited for their guests to arrive.

I never like it when my parents entertain. I hate sitting around in the afternoon looking at that sandwich meat all neatly rolled up and stabbed with toothpicks. Guacamole dip makes me want to gag. And why put out bowls and bowls of cashews and candies if you're not supposed to eat them?

Dinner itself isn't much better. I can't really enjoy the food. That white tablecloth glares at me, daring me to spill one drop of gravy, and the glasses are so thin I'm afraid I'm going to shatter mine just by picking it up.

I sat upstairs and sweltered because it was better than going down before it was absolutely necessary. It wasn't until four o'clock that I heard the doorbell ring and all those awkward introductions that follow. I shut my door tight and turned up the music. They would have to come get me.

A couple minutes later there was a knock on the door. "Joe," my mother sang out in a voice she only uses when we have company, "our guests are here."

I crawled downstairs, dreading the six hours I would have to spend with my nice new friend. But when I opened the French doors and went into the living room, there was John Lustik sprawled out in the overstuffed chair near the door. I couldn't believe my luck!

True, he was a little dull — Ross was right about that. But at least he played ball, at least he knew how to run and sweat and swear. That was more than I could say for Chucky.

Our parents went berserk with joy over the fact that we knew one another. Then I grabbed my basketball and we headed for the courts.

We were both dressed up a bit. I had on fancy jeans and a pin-striped shirt with a collar. John was wearing nylon Adidas warm-up pants and a long-sleeved T-shirt. A game didn't seem quite right, so we just shot around.

That got old fast. John suggested we play horse and I agreed. It was no contest. I crushed him with my outside jumper and my spinning inside shovel shots. All he could do was sink little jump shots from inside ten feet. Those shots were great in games, but with no one guarding me I matched him shot for shot.

For all his perfect manners, John hated to lose, even in horse. He didn't slam the ball down, or call me lucky, or want to switch to a different game. Instead, when I'd finished him off he'd immediately say, "Let's play another." He wanted to wipe the loss right out of his mind. For the first time, I found myself actually liking him.

I beat John six times in a row before we headed back. We had timed it just right. Our parents were ready to sit down and eat. We had missed all the boring chitchat.

Dinner started off great. My father tipped over his wine glass as he was filling it. It didn't break, but that red stain and those paper napkins shoved under the tablecloth put me at ease.

John's father wasn't half bad either. When he found out what my mother did he made a couple of dirty jokes, until his wife glared at him.

The whole thing should have gone fine, and it would have, if it hadn't been for my father. But he has a sneaky way of getting at things he thinks are important. His method is simple: he acts as if he could care less. So just when I finally thought that nothing could go wrong my father said, real casually, "John, why don't you tell Joe a little about Eastside Academy."

So off John went, singing the praises of good old Eastside. First he talked about National Merit scholars and SAT scores and college scholarships. I nodded but didn't say anything. Then he switched to the social aspect — dances and all that. Finally he got to basketball. "We've actually got an excellent team coming back. With you, we could probably take the league."

It was awful, listening to him saying all the right things about this perfect school I didn't want to go to. I could feel my father's eyes on me making sure I was paying close attention. I half expected him to jump on the table and scream, "You've got to go to Eastside! You've got to go to Eastside!"

John wasn't my favorite person in the world at that moment, but I didn't hate him. Not yet. After all, you really couldn't blame him for bragging about his school. Besides, he wasn't like me. He was content to be the perfect son in a perfect family, happy to slide on greased rails to fortune and success.

So I let John rattle on. And when he finished talking about basketball, I thought the whole unpleasant affair was over. But my father wasn't done. He had just fired one barrel. Ten minutes later, over dessert, he fired again.

"John," he said as he separated the chocolate icing from the cake, "we hear — or used to hear — a lot about a boy named Ross. We've never met him, but Joe seems quite taken with him. He must be quite a guy."

I knew John didn't like Ross. Ross was always on him, telling him how boring he was and all that. But I expect people my age to be able to tell when adults are poking in where they don't belong. So I figured John would spit out some formula, like "Ross is OK," and let the whole thing drop. That's what I would have done.

But not John. Dull, boring John picked that moment to get exciting. "Dr. Faust, Joe doesn't know Ross as well as I do. When you first meet him, Ross seems fine. But I think he's bad news. He's a great basketball player, but he's also a bully and a thief. He's got a slight chance of ending up in the NBA, but a much better chance of ending up in jail. I stay clear."

I couldn't believe it. This dimwit who never joked, never even smiled, had the nerve to trash Ross, who was ten times more alive than John could ever dream of being.

I couldn't let it go. My heart was pounding, my throat was tight, but I said it. I stood up and told John that he was a warm, wet piece of dung. Only I didn't use that word.

My moment of glory undoubtedly caused quite a bit of embarrassment for my parents. I'm sure rivers of apologies flowed. I didn't hear them. I had been banished to my room as punishment. Some punishment! Getting away from them suited me fine.

It was dusk. The windows were wide open and the room had cooled off. I pressed my face against the cold glass and the chill felt good on my cheek. Then I flopped down on my bed.

I knew I couldn't turn the stereo on without risking an explosion from my parents, and my subscription to *Sports Illustrated* hadn't started yet, so the only thing I had to look at were the books my father had gotten me. And the only one of those that interested me at all was *Dr. Faustus*.

I read a little here and there, and more of the story came back. Faustus is this famous medieval doctor — the smartest man in the world. That's not enough for him, though. He'll do anything for even more power, and I mean anything.

In school they tell you that the name "Smith" was given to the village blacksmith, and that "Taylor" was given to people who sewed. When I closed the book that evening, it struck me how weird it was to be named after someone who made a pact with the devil. There aren't many people with my name. And if Dr. Faustus were a person who really lived, and the book said that he did, then it was possible he was an ancestor of mine. I didn't know whether to be proud or ashamed.

9

The next morning my father came up to my room and we had one of our typically pointless conversations.

"What do you have to say for yourself?" he asked.

"Nothing that would do any good."

"Why don't you give it a try?"

"Well, I'm sorry I embarrassed you. Only . . . "
I stopped.

He sat down in the chair across from me. "Go on. I'm listening."

"Only nothing would have happened if you hadn't brought up Ross."

He lit a cigarette and smoked silently for a moment as he stared out the window. "Joe, I'm your father. I care about you, I care about what you're doing. Since we've been in Seattle you've spent all your time with Ross. I've never met him and neither has your mother. You won't bring him here, you won't tell us where you're going, what you're doing. What am I supposed to do?"

"I'm seventeen years old. Next year I'll be in college. You're supposed to trust me."

"I've always trusted you, Joe. But that's because you've always earned my trust. But now you're acting differently, as if you're hiding something. And people only hide when they've done something wrong."

I didn't know what to say, so I didn't say anything. He finished his cigarette and then told me I was to stay in my room all week. I didn't argue. He felt he had to punish me, so he did. That I could understand.

Even though I couldn't play basketball that week, I could watch the games from my window. I thought about how much things had changed since we'd first moved to Seattle, when I'd first looked out on those courts and the players had just been ants scurrying about. They existed miles away.

Now everything was closer. They weren't ants, but people. And the games were more than just a bunch of players running and shooting. The players were like soldiers, with John and Ross as opposing generals.

The more I watched, the more I realized that John was what my father wanted me to be. John always chose the safest option, the high-percentage play. Most people would say that's the smart way to do it. You win a fair share of games that way. But sometimes it takes more. Sometimes you have to be a little loose and a little wild.

Like Ross. Twisting in midair, he'd improvise shots, make up new moves, try unbelievable passes. When everything clicked, the result was a thing of beauty. The whole team would get a lift, and John's team would sink. Ross could make you feel that basketball was more than a robot game of pass and cut, screen and roll, box out and rebound. He made you feel that even though it was played on a little court, basketball was somehow infinite.

I was dying to get back out there, to be part of it again.

That week wouldn't end. The only time I saw my parents was at dinner. "Please pass the salt," was about all I said. "There you are," was about all my mother or father said. But on the last night before I was turned loose again, my father told me that he'd had a long talk with John's father.

"I explained to him you were sorry for what you said. That's true, isn't it?"

"Yes."

"Apparently John blames himself a little bit, too. He thinks maybe he said too much."

I nodded. "Maybe he did."

My father looked pleased. I hoped he would just drop the whole subject, but he didn't. There was a short pause, and then he started in again.

"John seems like a nice kid."

"He's all right."

"He seems bright, athletic, personable — he's got everything you could want in a friend."

"John's OK. I've got nothing against him. I just never hit it off with him. I don't know why. I just never did."

It was the wrong thing to say. "But did you ever try?"

I shook my head. "No, I guess I never really did."

"Well, do you think you should try?"

He was in a black mood. It was not the time to argue. "I'll try. I promise."

"Do you mean that?"

"Yes. I mean it."

10

The next morning I ate breakfast and headed straight to the courts. I was there by nine o'clock. I wanted to shoot around a bit by myself, get the feel back. My stomach churned when I thought about having to explain where I'd been. I decided to lie and say that I'd gone on vacation with my family. But nobody asked me anything, not even Ross. We picked teams and it was as if I'd never been gone.

My game was off a little, and John's team beat us 50–40. We played again, and they took us by twelve. We played three more games and my team won once. Then an odd thing happened. I was standing at the water fountain waiting my turn when John asked me if I wanted to shoot some pool in his basement. As John was talking, Ross came up. "Joe's not shooting any pool today, John. We're going to Green Lake to watch the girls jiggle as they run around the lake. Joe likes that. Right, Joe?"

The next thing I knew Ross had grabbed me by the arm and was sort of playfully pulling me along with him as he headed toward the bus stop. I looked back at John. "Maybe some other time," I yelled.

"Yeah," John called after me. "Some other time."

But he didn't ask me again. A couple of times I thought about asking John to come with Ross and me when we went downtown to the Pike Place Market. I figured it was something John would like to do. But Ross didn't want him. "He's such a drag!" So for the rest of the summer I only saw John on the basketball court and we were always on opposite teams.

Basket followed basket; game followed game. The days went by one after the other. One morning there was a thundershower. After that, the court was often wet from morning drizzle. The wind was blowing harder, too. Sometimes it was so stiff that it was hard to sink anything from outside ten feet. August was nearly over. Summer was drifting into fall.

11

Fall meant school and I still wasn't enrolled anywhere. Early one Tuesday morning my father put on his sport coat with the leather patches on the elbows and said he was taking the day off. "We'll go look at both Loyal High and at Eastside Academy, and then we'll make a decision."

It wasn't hard to look at Loyal High since it was two blocks away. As we left the house, I told my parents that I could walk to everything — games, dances, the school play — everything. "I wouldn't be borrowing the car."

My mother nudged my father. "Did you hear that? If we let him go to Loyal he won't ever ask to borrow the car." They both laughed.

"Well, hardly at all," I said, feeling foolish.

I kept quiet until we were actually on the school grounds. Then I tried again.

"This place has character. Look at the detail in the woodwork. And I think the paint job is really classy."

Of course, my father noticed the obscenities spray painted on a side wall. "You'd think they'd clean that up, wouldn't you?"

I pointed to the playing fields. "They've got six basketball courts, two football fields, and two baseball diamonds. I even think there's a soccer field out there somewhere. There are a lot more fields than Emerson ever had."

"It is quite large," my mother said.

But my father was unimpressed. "There's a lot of land, and the grounds could be nice. But those rims are bent, and the fields are just hardpan and weeds. I wouldn't want to get tackled out there."

For the next ten minutes we walked around the school. I knew my father hated the place, but it was useless to try to change his mind so I didn't say a thing. When we returned to the main entrance, my parents started up the stairs.

"I'm sure the building is closed," I said. "There won't be anybody there."

My father motioned for me to follow him. "There had better be somebody here. We made an appointment to speak with the principal." I looked at my mother and she shrugged. They could have told me.

We trooped up two long flights of stairs and my

father pounded on the old wooden door. We waited for a long time before an old, grizzled janitor came and opened the door a crack.

"I'm Dr. Faust. I've made an appointment to speak with Ms. Jefferson."

The janitor screwed up his face and rubbed the stubble on his chin. "Nyra ain't here. Ain't nobody here but me. It's summer, buddy."

"I spoke with her just last week. The appointment was for nine o'clock. If you don't mind, we'll wait in the lobby."

"Suit yourself," the janitor answered as he wiped his mouth with a dirty handkerchief, "but I can tell you right now that there is no way in hell Nyra's going to be here at nine." Then he snickered. "Mister, she don't even come at nine when there is school."

We waited forty-five minutes. Nyra Jefferson never showed up, never called. My father found the janitor and asked him to inform Ms. Jefferson that we had been there.

"Do I look like a secretary, Jack? You got something to tell Nyra, you tell her yourself."

So ended our visit to Loyal High.

It took an hour to get to Eastside because of an accident on the Evergreen Floating Bridge. I could just picture myself stuck on a bus with a bunch of eggheads discussing the lead article in *Scientific American* and the latest breakthrough in home computers. As we sweated our way across the bridge, my father went on about the view of the Cascade

Mountains and how wonderful it would be to see sunrises over the lake.

"That would be nice, wouldn't it?" my mother agreed. I didn't say a word.

Eastside was big, but other than that it was just like Emerson, clean and old. All the brick buildings had ivy crawling up the walls. Cherry trees lined the pathways. "Look at those dahlias," my mother said. "And the rose garden!"

Behind the main building were green playing fields with a creek running through them. The school was perfect, like out of some old dusty book.

I hated it.

It's not that I wanted to do drugs, or stop studying, or anything like that. I wanted to learn; I wanted to go to college. But I also wanted to go to a normal high school where the principal wouldn't call your parents if a pack of cigarettes was found in your locker, where I wouldn't have to tuck in my shirt, and where I might meet some girls who didn't button their blouses up to their chins. I didn't really care whether the science lab was the best. I wanted to go to a school where the basketball was the best. But how could I explain that to my father?

After we had strolled around the grounds, we again climbed stairs to a school office. Of course the principal, Mr. Rowe, was waiting for us. He had on a coat and tie and he sat in front of a wall of books. He was delighted to meet me, my father, my mother. He was proud to discuss Eastside students' scholarships, college grade-point averages, all that stuff. "More than half of our teachers have advanced degrees," he cooed, "and our physics teacher has his doctorate." My father looked at my mother and nodded approvingly. She nodded back. Nobody so much as glanced at me.

When we reached home, we talked calmly for a bit. Then it turned ugly. I told my father I'd flunk out of Eastside on purpose. He screamed that I'd learn more failing at Eastside than I would getting straight A's at Loyal High. It went on like that for about ten minutes, him yelling and me yelling back. My mother didn't say much of anything, but finally she brought it to a halt. "I have a model coming, so let's stop for today. We'll sleep on it and talk again tomorrow."

12

I couldn't sleep that night. I kept going over the argument I'd had with my father, trying to think of things I should have said. That's why I heard my parents fighting.

It was after midnight when the light went on in their bedroom. Then I heard my father pacing back and forth. I slipped out of bed, went over to my door, opened it a crack, and listened.

I couldn't hear much, just bits of things. I heard my mother say Ross's name, then my father said something about Stanford. Then it seemed like they were both talking at once. Next I heard my mother almost shout, "For once, will you listen to me?" After that, they were silent. I thought maybe they were done, but they started again, only this time they were whispering and I couldn't make out a word. The next thing I knew their door opened and the stairway was flooded with light. I closed my door and hustled back to bed. I recognized my mother's footsteps on the stairs.

There was a light tap at the door. I thought about pretending to be asleep, but then she tapped again and opened the door.

"Are you awake? Can I come in?"

"Sure," I whispered, and I faked a yawn. "I'm awake."

She came and sat on the bed next to me. The night was still and dark.

"Tell me why you want to go to Loyal High. Honest and truly."

I didn't know where to start. But then I thought about how much I wanted to play in the same back-court with Ross, and the words came. "I know you and Dad think this is stupid, but I really want to play Metro basketball. It's the best league in the state, and I'll never know how good I am unless I play in it. I may not even make the team at Loyal High, but at least I'll know. If I go to Eastside, I'll be on some hokey team in some hokey league where the guys don't really care."

"So it's entirely because of basketball that you want to go to Loyal?"

"There are other things, too. Only they're harder to explain. I want to meet different kinds of people, I guess. All the people at places like Eastside are the same."

She stopped me there. "Tell me this, do you honestly think that Ross is a good person for you, a good friend?"

I'd never really thought about him like that before. I knew I couldn't just say "Yes" because it was more complicated than that. "I'm not really sure," I finally answered. "I don't like everything about him, but I like him. He's different from anybody I've ever known. But he's not going to get me in trouble, if that's what you're worried about. I can look after myself."

"He's exciting to be around, is that what you mean?"

I thought of the basketball games and the night on the golf course. "Yeah, I guess that's it."

In the moonlight I saw her smile, a warm wonderful smile. Then she told me a story that embarrassed me a little, though I can see why she told it. She said that when she was in high school her parents were very strict and kept a close eye on her every move. "The Senior Ball was coming up and I begged my mother to let me pick my dress all by myself. It took hours of arguing — that's how protective my parents were — but finally my mother agreed. I went to the department store and picked out an off-white dress with a plunging neckline. I wanted a little excitement in my life, too. I took that dress home and my mother forced me to try it on for her. When she saw me in it, she was shocked. She marched me down to the store and made me return it. She said that I'd thank her for it later."

"So?" I said, afraid that she'd tell me I'd thank her later for packing me off to Eastside.

"So my mother was wrong. She should have let me wear that dress."

Then my mother kissed me on the forehead and left.

When I awoke, the sunlight was streaming in through the windows. There were sailboats out on the Sound, some with colorful spinnakers like rainbows. Huge freighters, primer orange, were being tugged out to deep water. It was such a great morning that it made me glad to be in Seattle. Then I remembered Eastside, and it was all I could do to drag myself downstairs.

My parents were drinking coffee in the kitchen. I poured myself a bowl of cereal and sat down at the table. My father looked up from the newspaper.

"Well, Joe, you've seen both schools. You're old enough to make up your mind. So which school will it be?"

I froze.

My mother smiled at me. "Do you need more time to make up your mind?"

"No," I sputtered, trying to fight down the excitement that was creeping into my voice. "I want to go to Loyal High."

My father looked at me for a long time. Then he looked at my mother. "Good, I'm glad that's settled. Now I have to get to the lab. I missed a lot of work yesterday."

He stood up, but before he left the kitchen he looked me in the eye. "I know I can trust you anywhere."

"That's right, Dad, you can trust me." I looked over at my mother. "You can trust me," I repeated, this time for her.

I could hear my father packing up his stuff for work. The front door opened, but instead of leaving, he came back to the kitchen. I was afraid he'd changed his mind.

"I couldn't help noticing you've been reading *Dr. Faustus,*" he said. "I hope you'll still finish. Who knows, it might be on Loyal High's reading list, if they have one."

I nodded. "I'll finish it. I'm actually enjoying it."

A few seconds later the door closed behind him and he was gone. I could breathe easy again.

13

When I went outside that morning, it was all I could do to keep from going crazy with joy. And when I saw the guys on the court, I wanted to scream that a miracle had taken place. But all along I had told everybody that I was going to Loyal High. My news was no news to them. That didn't stop the blood from pumping through my body like water from a hydrant.

All that adrenalin had to come out somewhere, and it did — in the basketball game. It wasn't just that I shot well. I've had lots of games where I was hot, where almost every jump shot tickled the net. This time it was different. The passes I made had zip, yet when they arrived it was as if they had floated in, soft and quiet, like a lost balloon. When I jumped, I had the extra inch I needed to wrestle the tough rebounds from everyone. I even had a quick first step, so the loose balls came my way.

But the most amazing thing was the way in which it fell together. I knew exactly when to pass and when to shoot, when to cut back on the fast break and when to go baseline.

We jumped out to a 10–2 lead. John hit a couple of buckets and they closed it to 14–10. Then a steal, an outside jumper, and a quick outlet pass to Ross pushed it back to 20–10. Usually there's a letdown when you get up early in a game, but not this time. I kept the pressure on, the baskets kept coming, and the score mounted. 30–14 . . . 42–22 . . . 48–28 . . .

It happened on the last basket. I anticipated a pass to John and cut in front of him. I tipped the ball out into the open court and raced in front of everyone. My legs felt like rockets. I took the ball straight to the hole and went up and up and up. I hadn't thought about it before; I hadn't thought at all during the whole game. Everything had just happened. This just happened, too. I kept going up, kept soaring so high that suddenly the rim was below and — unbelievably — I found myself slam-dunking the ball through the hoop. It was impossible — I didn't have enough vertical leap to do it — but I had done it!

The guys just stared at me for a moment. Then they all came rushing up, giving me high-fives, slapping and shaking me so hard that the spell was broken. I came out of it and it was like saying good-bye to another person.

The guys all prodded me to do it again, especially Ross. I didn't want to try. I knew I couldn't do it again, at least not then. Besides, I suddenly felt exhausted. I was happy, but very, very tired.

We shot around for a few minutes and I thought it was over. Then Ross fired a hard chest pass at me. "Let's see you do it again, Joe."

"What's the big deal, Ross? I told you I don't feel like it."

"No big deal, Joe. I just think it was a fluke. Stuff it once more and I'll keep my mouth shut."

The other guys were staring at me. I had no choice. I backed up to half court, took a deep breath, and drove to the hoop. The feeling was completely gone.

My legs were heavy and the basket seemed to rise above me as I jumped. The ball jammed against the front rim and the force knocked me flat on my back. All the guys laughed.

I was angry as I regained my feet, angry at making a fool of myself, angry at having my magic moment spoiled by this stupid second try that I hadn't wanted to take.

Ross chased down the ball, dribbled it between his legs a few times, made some joke about my dunk, and then netted a jump shot. I didn't even make a move for the ball. No one did. We all knew what was going to happen.

Ross picked the ball up, backed up to half court, and took sight on the rim. He gathered up his strength, pulled together his concentration. Then he came, like a whirlwind. Four hard dribbles and he took off, arm outstretched, the ball climbing until it was just above the rim, and then down and through. He had matched me. I knew the wild joy he felt. I knew the feeling because he had stolen it from me.

14

I didn't do anything with Ross that afternoon. I went straight home. My back hurt and I had a good-sized lump on my head. The next morning I was so stiff I could hardly walk, let alone play. I stayed in that day.

I figured I'd better read at least a little of *Dr. Faustus*. There's only so much you can get from the pictures, and I was afraid my father was going to ask me about it again. Things were sailing along nicely, and I didn't want to screw up. So I sat by the window and read.

I didn't understand all of it, probably because I just skimmed the long speeches, but I got the gist of the first twenty pages. It's set in the Middle Ages. The main character, Faustus, is an expert at everything. He knows all there is to know about logic, philosophy, and even religion. But even though he's the most brilliant guy alive, he's miserable. He feels none of his knowledge amounts to anything.

That's a lot like my father. My father would work at some problem for months, and when he'd solved it, he'd insist it wasn't that important, that it didn't really matter. I figured it was false modesty, but reading *Dr. Faustus* made me think my father might not be a hypocrite. Maybe lots of smart people are depressed.

Anyway, I'd just gotten to the part where Faustus calls out to the devil when my mother yelled my name and asked for help cutting up the greens for the dinner salad. I can't say I was crushed to have my reading interrupted. I figured I'd read enough to get by if my father asked me anything.

The next morning the sun was shining, my head didn't ache, and sitting inside was not high on my list of things to do. I was still mad at Ross, but when he saw me he gave me a big smile. "Hey, we missed you yesterday." And during the games he did everything he could to get me points. A few hoops always make a basketball player happy, and Ross knew it. He had a way about him; I never could stay mad at him for long.

As we walked down to Shilshole Bay after the games broke up, Ross told me about a party he was giving, a "last blast" before school started again. "You'll meet the guys from Loyal, and some of the girls, too. You've got to come."

All my Boston friends were like me — well chaperoned. Of course, we drank beer whenever we could get it, and some of the guys smoked a little grass. But it was always a big deal, always on the sly down by the river at night or behind the farthest playing field in the late afternoon. We had parties, but they were the well-organized kind, the kind where you wore slacks and said good-bye to the host's mother before you settled into your mother's waiting car.

I knew Ross was talking about something entirely different. His parents would be gone. The refrigerator would be full of Rainier beer and there were hints of more exotic stimulants. The girls, to hear him tell it, were accustomed to life on the wild side. He was sure they'd be glad to meet me.

I sure wanted to meet them.

The problem was pulling it off. My parents had always made it a point to meet the parents of my friends before they'd allow me to go to any parties.

They wanted to be sure I'd be in the right environment, as they put it.

Ross's parents weren't like that. They'd think nothing of going to Reno over the weekend and leaving him home alone. They even told him they didn't care what he did so long as the police didn't come and he cleaned up afterward. There was no way they'd sip tea and eat croissants with my parents.

I hoped to slip it by them. "Ross is having a party Saturday night," I said one morning at breakfast. "I think I might just stop by for an hour or two."

"That sounds nice," my mother said. "School's starting up. There won't be much time for parties then."

"True enough," I said, trying to get out the door.

"You know," my father said, "your mother and I still haven't met either Ross or his parents. How about if we have them over some evening for a little ice cream and cake? If they're putting on a big party, it's the least we could do."

I wanted to scream. It was the same old stuff. "Dad, this isn't Boston. This is the West Coast. People don't do things like that here."

He stared at me. "People don't have friends over for ice cream and cake on the West Coast?"

"People aren't so formal here. I can go to Ross's party without you meeting his parents. It's no big deal. Actually, they'd think it was weird if you invited them over."

"Joe," my mother said, "I can hardly believe that Ross's parents would think it was weird if we had them over for dessert. Now why don't you tell us what the real problem is?"

I sat down again. I had to think how to say it the best way. I started out by telling them that Ross's father was out of work. "From what I understand," I continued, "he also drinks too much. Anyway, I know it would make him feel bad to come here into this house and meet you."

My father and mother were both silent. Finally my mother said, "I'm sure that being out of work would hurt a man's pride. Your father and I would never want to embarrass anyone. We'll meet Ross's parents some other time. But I do think it's time we met Ross, don't you?"

There was no way I could talk them out of that.

It took some doing, but I made Ross agree to come over for lunch on the Saturday of the party. I lived that week in dread.

I paced around Saturday morning wondering if Ross would really come. When noon came and he didn't, part of me was relieved. He finally showed up at twelve-forty wearing cutoff jeans and an Adam Ant T-shirt. I could feel my parents exchanging glances.

We shuffled into the front room and tried to talk. Mostly there was awkward silence. Ross answered my parents' questions with Yeah's and Na's. Occasionally he managed a half sentence.

We ate in the breakfast room. Ross wolfed down two ham and cheese sandwiches. I couldn't finish my first one.

The conversation turned to Loyal High. Ross grew excited at last. "We've got a great team. If Joe feeds me enough passes, I might take the scoring title and make all-league."

"What are your plans for next year?" my mother asked. "Will you go on to college?"

Ross laughed out loud. I wish I had a picture of the expression on my parents' faces.

"Me? College? I suppose if some school gave me a new car, the names of some fast girls, and a long list of Mickey Mouse courses, I'd think about it. Otherwise, no way, José!"

That was the worst of it. Ross stayed until one forty-five. "Thanks a lot," he mumbled as he left. "Lunch was great."

When the door closed, I stood there, waiting. I knew they didn't like Ross, but neither of them said a word. I guess they were sick of fighting me. Anyway, I'd met their one condition. I could go to the party. That was all I cared about.

15

Ross lived off 20th Avenue on N.W. 58th Street, about a mile from Sunset Hill. The homes in Ballard are set out on a grid, so it was easy to find.

Once you crossed 24th Avenue, the houses were closer together and a little run-down. Lots of the lawns were overgrown and full of weeds. People hung underwear on the lines in the backyards. It was different from Sunset Hill. It made me mad that I noticed the little things.

Ross's house wasn't that much worse than the others on his block. It looked like it had seen better days, but it wasn't a dump like John had said. The paint was hardly peeling. The porch steps were tilted and rotting, but there wasn't garbage in the back-yard or litter strewn along the driveway.

I walked up the porch steps, took a deep breath, and knocked on the door. I could hear U2 on the stereo, but no one opened up. So I knocked again, louder. I heard, or thought I heard, a muffled "It's open."

I turned the knob and stepped inside. There was so much smoke and so little light that it took me a while to make out what was what. On the couch one guy had his hands all over this dark-haired girl, beer cans were lying on the floor, and a big black dog was huddled in the corner.

I felt lost. My first impulse was to go right back out again. But I just stood in the doorway.

Finally I saw Ross. He was coming out of the kitchen, a bottle of wine in one hand and a cigarette in the other. He was laughing with a blond girl, then he saw me out and motioned me over.

Getting to him took some doing, but when I finally reached him he slapped a beer in my hand and told me there was only one rule: "Keep the door closed and the windows shut. Otherwise the neighbors get uptight and call the police." I nodded and said I understood, but I was hardly listening. I couldn't take my eyes off the girl.

Ross noticed. "This is Karen. I've been telling her about you." Then he gave me a friendly dig in the ribs, winked, and walked away.

Karen was a knockout. Her hair was strawberry blond and she had light blue eyes. She wore cutoff blue jeans and a pink halter top that she filled quite nicely. I started to like the party.

I admit that at first I was mainly interested in Karen's body, but after we talked for a while — and drank for a while — I found out there was more to her. It turned out she wrote poetry and was deeply concerned about the treatment of blacks in South Africa. "Some days I get so depressed I just break down and cry." I took her hand when she said that.

I told her I knew how she felt, that sometimes I stared out the window at night and thought about how far away the stars are and about how deep and silent the bottom of the ocean must be.

Karen and I went on talking and drinking beer for the next three hours. I started to wish we had talked more and drank less. By midnight the room was swaying and my eyes felt like they were covered with Vaseline.

I got the brilliant idea that dancing would make

me feel better. Right away I knew something was seriously wrong. It was a slow song. I had this beautiful blond wrapped up in my arms, but I didn't feel anything except sick. I managed to convince Karen that we should return to the sofa. She snuggled up close and started kissing my neck. It was the opportunity of a lifetime, but with every passing second I felt worse and worse. I reached behind me and threw open all the windows I could reach. Not even fresh air helped. My head was pounding; my eyes were burning; my stomach was turning over.

I had to get outside, and quick! Prying myself free from Karen, I staggered across the room, opened the front door, stumbled down the stairs, and vomited on the lawn. Then I passed out cold.

Well, not quite cold. I have a dim memory of the police car pulling up in front of Ross's house, of the music suddenly turning into silence, and of kids scurrying by me. But it's as if all that took place at the bottom of a deep lake and I were watching it from a boat rocking on the surface above. Then came a ride in a police car, a knock on a door, and my father and mother in their robes on the front porch.

The next thing I knew it was morning. The sun burned in through the east window. My mouth felt like a desert and my head pounded. I lay flat on my back and stared at my poster of Magic Johnson.

At breakfast there were red roses on the kitchen table and a bowl of blueberries next to them. My father was munching his Grape-Nuts and my mother was sipping her coffee. Neither of them looked up when I entered. It wasn't until I poured myself some orange juice that my mother spoke.

"Joseph, your father and I have decided that you will attend Eastside Academy. Also, from this day on you are to have nothing to do with Ross. The reasons for both of these steps are obvious, so there will be no discussion. Is that clear?"

It was clear. I went back upstairs and lay down. I felt so awful I didn't get up again until after two, and it wasn't until three o'clock that I dug my ball out of the closet and drifted over to Loyal High to shoot around. It was strange walking past that old building, knowing I wouldn't be going there.

I hadn't been shooting for long when Ross showed up. I can't say I was surprised; I had a feeling he'd be there.

"I'm sorry," I said. "I hope I didn't get you into too much trouble."

He shrugged. "Don't worry about it. The police didn't do anything to me. They'll chew out my old man when he gets back tomorrow, and then he'll chew me out, and it'll be over. How did it go at your house?"

"Not so good. My father's making me go to Eastside now."

"And you're going to do it?"

"What choice do I have?"

Ross bounced his ball a few times. "You know,

Joe, you don't have to do what he says. Just register tomorrow at Loyal. You're seventeen. He can't stop you."

"It's not that simple, Ross."

"Sure it is. What's he going to do — make you drop out?"

We shot around for a few minutes, but my head started to ache again. I picked up my ball and drifted off. I was about a hundred yards away when Ross called my name. I turned back to him.

"See you at school tomorrow," he shouted.

For the rest of the day I kept thinking about what Ross had said. I knew he was right — my parents couldn't stop me. All I had to do was face up to them. But I didn't. I meant to — I kept telling myself I was going to take them on. But I never said a word.

PART
TWO

PART

TWO

1

September 3 — the first day of my last year of high
school. The bus didn't reach my stop until seven-
thirty, but I was up at six. All I could see out the
windows was fog. No mountains, no lakes, no
houses — just gray, wet fog.

At least I didn't have to wear a shirt with a collar
like in Boston. Eastside's only dress rule was that
cutoffs were forbidden. I put on my new blue jeans,
tucked in my new polo shirt, laced up my new leather
basketball shoes, and tiptoed to the bathroom.

I wanted to be out of the house before my parents
awoke, so I tried hard to be quiet. I knocked over
the plastic cup in the bathroom and it clattered
around in the sink, but other than that I washed up
without making much noise.

I slipped downstairs into the kitchen, fried myself
two eggs, and plunked them down on two pieces

of toast. I ate fast, chugged some orange juice from the carton, took my lunch out of the refrigerator, and headed for the front door.

I didn't make it. My mother was halfway down the stairs in her robe. "A little early, aren't you?" she whispered as she fought off her early-morning drowsiness.

"A little, but I don't want to miss the bus."

"I see." She smiled. I climbed the stairs and gave her a good-bye kiss. "It won't be all bad," she said.

She was right, though it did have some terrible moments. The first one came right away. They have all of Sunset Hill to find a place for the crummy bus to stop, so where do they choose? Right in front of the 7–Eleven where the Loyal High kids hang out smoking cigarettes and eating candy.

I can't say anybody razzed me, but that might be because I never raised my head. I just stared at the garbage in the gutter and prayed that the bus would come.

It was only ten minutes late, but it seemed like an hour. I climbed the three steps and found myself facing twenty strangers. Then I saw John. He nodded to me and I nodded back. He moved his stuff over.

"I thought you were going to Loyal," he said when I sat down next to him.

"I thought so, too, but my parents pulled the plug on that idea."

"Eastside's not so bad. You'll see."

We didn't talk much after that. John never had much to say, and I was tired and depressed.

We were quiet, but the bus wasn't. By the time we reached the Evergreen Floating Bridge, it was full. Most of the kids knew one another, so there was a lot of "How you been?" and "Where did you go on your vacation?"

The answers made me want to throw up. It was the same old story — rich kids telling other rich kids about their rich-kid vacations. "We went to Paris." "Oh, I've been there. Don't you find the French insufferable?" . . . "It's too hot in Acapulco in summer. My mother said we must go back over Christmas break." . . . "The Orient is so strange, so mysterious. It makes one feel the limitations of Western culture."

The bus filled up with this nonstop chatter, the same type of chatter I'd heard for years, only without the Boston accents. I wondered if I was going to have to hear it my whole life.

When I stepped off the bus, I was glad I knew John. Eastside was much bigger than Emerson. I was a late registrant, and I didn't know where to go. "You'll pick up your registration package at Bailey Hall" — he pointed to one building — "and you'll get your locker and your P.E. stuff over at Crandon. After that, you need to go — " He stopped. He must have sensed my confusion. "Look, why don't I just show you."

Even with his help it took a solid twenty minutes

to get everything done. The warning bell rang and I had to hustle not to be late.

2

The teachers at Eastside were pretty much like the ones in Boston — either strange or boring. Some of them were both strange *and* boring. I had Mr. Kerry for homeroom and history. "Keep off my wall," he shrieked in the first two minutes. We eventually figured out he was screaming at a pimply-faced loser who was leaning against the side wall. The poor guy was so embarrassed his whole face turned red.

Kerry spent the rest of the period reliving his war years. "I was in the bloodiest action in Korea," he bragged. "Sometimes, in the heat of battle, we'd spin that tank on a dime. If some Red was in the way, too bad. Later we'd go back and check out the surprised look smashed on his face." Kerry promised to be entertaining, if not truthful.

Second period was another story. Mr. Anyati was a refugee from Khomeini and had once been a light-heavyweight Olympic boxer for Iran. He taught Math IV: Preparation for College. Anyati spoke with a thick Iranian accent. He called on one guy named Sampson, who didn't understand the question and giggled out of nervousness. Anyati threw a fit, started yammering in whatever language Iranians speak, and finally forced Sampson to get down on his knees. I was glad I'd always been good in math.

After math came physics with Dr. Elmer. He spoke so softly you had to be real quiet to hear. Nobody felt like being real quiet, so nobody heard anything. Elmer didn't seem to notice all the talking and laughing going on. Somebody whispered that he had a hole in his head. Sure enough, when I looked closely I did see a tiny hole just above his right eye.

French was fourth period. You always hope your French teacher is going to be a knockout, but Mrs. Monbouquette was gray and dumpy. She gave us a test right away. It was a snap. Miss Boucher in Boston had worked us hard.

Next came lunch, which I ate alone by the back stairwell of the gym. It felt strange. In Boston I was always part of a group. Other kids knew me and liked me. I was on the basketball team; my grades were pretty good; my father was famous; my mother was a little infamous. I never thought about making friends, I just had them.

At Eastside I was nobody. I was a new kid in school. I'd seen new kids come to Emerson and never catch on with anyone. They just moped through a semester or a year and disappeared. As I ate my sandwich, I wondered if that was going to happen to me. I decided it didn't matter. I could just sit in the back of the class, take the grades that came my way, go home, listen to the stereo, and look out the window. I could survive a year of anything.

Then I heard the familiar thud of a basketball hitting pavement. John was heading toward the court with two other guys. They were laughing with one another. "I'm still two inches taller than you, Snellinger," John said.

"No way!" Snellinger shouted. They turned back to back. "Doyle, check this out." Doyle was a good four inches shorter than both of them. He tried to see who was taller, but Snellinger kept going up on his tiptoes.

"Cut that out!" John laughed and went up on his tiptoes.

Just then another guy came over. He sized up both Snellinger and John. "Hey, I think I'm taller than both of you wimps."

"In your dreams, Reynolds," John joked. "In your dreams."

The three of them finally did it fair and square. John was the tallest, but just by an inch. The other two were exactly the same height.

I didn't care who was the tallest, but I was amazed that this private school had three big horses and still wasn't a cinch to take the title. At Emerson, we didn't have one guy the size of John and we did all right.

They took the court and immediately broke into a little two-on-two. I walked up and stood underneath the hoop. After his team scored a bucket, John spotted me. "Joe," he said, "get somebody else so we can make this three-on-three." I nodded and

they went back to their game. I didn't know anybody. Where was I going to find another player?

I wandered over to the cafeteria. I wasted five
minutes feeling stupid and then went back to the
court. I had a vague hope that somebody else would
be standing around like I'd been.

The two-on-two half-court game had grown to
five-on-five, full-court. All the guys were fast or big,
or both. They played hard and they didn't call prissy
fouls. A player would have to be hammered before
he said a thing. They would have chewed up my
team at Emerson and spit us out on the gym floor.

I backed away from the court. I didn't want to
seem pathetic, but I had to watch. I studied the
guards the closest. Not one was Ross, but not one
was Bozo the Clown, either.

Two of them, Stamets and Burns, were adequate.
But Doyle was good. He could drive left; he could
stick the outside jumper. And Seth Sharkey, a red-
headed kid I recognized from French class, was even
better. He worked the ball around and made sure
everybody was involved. Sharkey knew when to
push the fast break and when to back off, and he
kept Alex Reynolds from losing his temper when a
play went sour. Sharkey even passed up open shots
to keep his teammates in the flow.

I got a knot in my stomach watching the game.
I'd assumed I was too good for Eastside. But these
guys were like a well-oiled machine, and I felt like
a spare part stuck on a shelf. With Sharkey playing

the point they didn't need me, no matter what John had said. I drifted back to the stairwell and waited for the bell.

My first afternoon class was English. It was the only class John and I had together, but all the seats around him were taken, so I sat alone toward the back.

The teacher's name was Miss Mitchell. She had dark, wavy hair and deep brown eyes. She wore a long skirt and a pink, pin-striped blouse. She seemed nervous as she stood in the front of the room and read off our names. I heard one of the kids whisper it was her first year of teaching. Miss Mitchell didn't look a whole lot older than the girls in the class, and she wore less makeup than most of them.

When she reached my name on the roll, she stopped.

"Faust — that's an unusual name. Do you know the legend about the German doctor?"

"I know the story. We've got the book at home and I've flipped through it a couple of times."

She smiled. "We're going to read Marlowe's play this semester — if the books ever arrive — and the Drama Club will put it on in February."

After roll call, that first day was all fun and games. Miss Mitchell went to the blackboard and wrote, "My dream had finally come true . . ." and gave us ten minutes to write on that theme.

She called on Eddie Doyle first. His story was

about a gorgeous redhead stripping while he watched. It wasn't very well written, and he mumbled when he spoke, but he had the anatomy right. We all snickered, even the girls, and watched Miss Mitchell for her reaction. She laughed too, and I knew right then that she was a good person, because most teachers won't laugh at anything that has to do with sex. I figured English wouldn't be so bad.

P.E. was the last class of the day. Mr. Raible was your classic Marine-turned-gym-teacher. He made us do twenty push-ups, and he came around and kicked the butts of the guys who couldn't keep their bodies straight. Then we did sixty sit-ups, climbed the ropes, did forward and backward rolls. Raible saved the worst for last — cartwheels. I'd never learned how to do them as a kid. Not many guys did, and Raible mocked them all.

"That was brutal!" he shouted after I had sort of flopped over on my back. I couldn't help laughing as I stood up.

"So you think being brutal is funny, do you?" Raible sneered.

"No, I don't. I just don't know how to do cartwheels."

"What do you say when you address me?" He looked furious and frightening. I stared at him, my mind blank.

"I don't know what you mean," I stammered.

"Then you don't know much, do you?"

"I guess not."

"You say 'sir' when you address me, understand?"

"Yes."

"Yes what?" he barked.

"Yes, sir."

As I was dressing after class, John came over to me. "Raible can be a real jerk, but try to get on his good side."

I had to laugh at that. "I'd love to be on his good side. I don't want that cretin torturing me all year."

John laughed. "You're not going to believe this, Joe, but that cretin isn't just your P.E. teacher, he's also the head basketball coach."

3

I killed the bus ride home by imagining what my first day would have been like back at Emerson if we hadn't moved. I pictured myself saying hello to all my buddies, checking in with Coach Anderson. Some of the teachers might even have welcomed me back. I could see myself giving the new girls the once-over, and checking out the other girls, too.

It was a pleasant daydream, but when I got off the bus at Sunset Hill I came back to reality fast. I had to go two blocks out of my way to avoid the Loyal High basketball courts. All I wanted to do was to slip inside the house, go to my room, turn on the stereo, and think.

When I turned the corner at 80th, I saw press cars and TV trucks in front of my house. My father was on the porch with twenty microphones catching his every word. I knew he must have once again done something stupendous, so I changed direction and headed for the back door.

I was almost in the house when I heard someone call my name. I turned around and saw a woman reporter who looked like Cybill Shepherd.

"You must be Dr. Faust's son," she said. "Did you know your father has just won the Albert Lasker Award?

"That's great," I said, and wondered why she wasn't out there listening to him.

She took off her glasses and smiled. "I'd like to talk with you for a few minutes, if you don't mind. My magazine is after the personal angle. 'A day in the life of a great scientist,' that sort of thing. You could help tremendously."

"You should talk to my mother."

"Oh, I will. I'll talk to both of them at the award ceremony in December. But you could get me started. It won't take long."

I had a vague feeling that something wasn't quite right. But I just couldn't get in the door. Everyone else was interested in my father, yet this beautiful woman wanted to talk to me.

We walked over to Sunset Hill Park and sat on

a bench overlooking the Sound. At first she asked me boring questions and I filled her in on boring details. I told her my father's schedule, his favorite TV shows, movies, records, books. I described how athletic he was. Just garbage like that.

She nodded. "It's great to hear a son praise his father. It really is. It's refreshing. But to tell you the truth, Joe, nobody's going to believe this if your family comes across as being perfect. The whole thing will sound phony."

I could see what she meant and figured it wouldn't hurt to tell her about some other stuff. But once she got me started, I couldn't stop. Practically every mean thing I've ever thought or heard about my father came spilling out. I told her about how he never came to my games. I told her that he wouldn't let me go to public school and that he wanted a perfect world filled with perfect people — people just like him. I told her everything. It was almost as if it wasn't me talking, not really. It was as if some power had taken over and was speaking through me. And so when she asked me about my mother, I kept right on babbling away.

"I get along really well with her, but I don't see her much because she's so busy with her work."

"What does your mother do?"

"She's an artist. She goes by the name of Ella Frank. You may have heard of her. She has a piece in the Metropolitan Museum of Art in New York, and she's had lots of shows in Boston."

"Where is her studio? I'd like to see her work."

I explained that my mother's studio was in the house, on the second floor.

The reporter looked puzzled. "I don't get it. I thought you said you don't see your mother much."

"Well, I don't usually go into her studio. The models make me uncomfortable and I don't think my mother wants me there."

The woman smiled. "I guess you don't like looking at naked girls."

"No, no!" I said. "That's not it. I don't mind naked girls. My mother has naked boys for models."

As soon as it came out I felt incredibly stupid. *I don't mind naked girls.* What kind of a thing was that to say?

Instead of laughing at me, the woman suddenly seemed very interested. "How do you avoid your mother's studio? It must be right in the middle of the house."

"My room is up in the attic away from the main house. It's not a bad room, though it was a little hot in the summer and it'll be damp in the winter. Still, when I'm up there I don't bother my mother."

She stood up. "You're a good kid, Joe. And you've been very helpful." She put out her hand and I shook it. Then she walked across the grass to a waiting Cadillac. I waved to her and she smiled and waved back. But just before she drove off, I thought I saw her take a tiny tape recorder out of her pocket.

By the time I reached the house, all the reporters

were gone. My mother and father were in the kitchen, talking excitedly. They both beamed when they saw me. My mother jumped up and hugged me. "Joe, we have great news! Your father has won the Lasker Award!"

When she let go, it was my father's turn. I tried to shake his hand and congratulate him man-to-man, but he pulled me to him and gave me a big hug and then lifted me up like I was a five-year-old. They were both so happy that it was impossible for me to hold out. I started smiling and laughing, too.

"There's one thing to remember," my father cautioned me later, when we had all calmed down a bit. "Many people object to my work on principle. They think the genetic code is sacred and recombining genes is evil. They've been slandering me for years, and this award will only make their attacks more vicious. So if anybody from the press happens to get in touch with you, watch what you say. Be polite, but be careful."

I froze. All I could think about was that tape being rewound and the sound of my voice filling some strange room full of strange people. They would hear the things I had said. I felt like I was going to choke, like my throat was going to close up. I excused myself and went to the bathroom and splashed cold water on my face.

The local news that night was full of my father. Reporters gushed over his genius. Gene-splicing would one day rid the world of everything from cystic fibrosis to gypsy moths. It would cure cancer and control diabetes. All of these miracles would be the result of the work of Seattle's newest and greatest scientific genius, Dr. Joseph Faust. My father blushed and insisted they were exaggerating, but I could tell how proud he was.

All my life I'd been told that he was a great scientist. But I always thought of science as something that stayed in the lab. Hearing what they said about him on TV that night made me realize that my father's work was part of something that was changing the world. Most of me was happy and proud, but I have to admit a part of me was depressed and jealous.

4

The Lasker Award changed things at school. I became a secondhand celebrity. Suddenly everyone knew me, and everyone wanted to know more — not about me, but about my father.

"Does he discuss his work with you?"

"Is he concerned about social issues?"

"How much money did he get?"

I repeated the same answers. My father was a great guy. He didn't discuss his work at home. He thought constantly about the practical applications of recombinant DNA. I didn't know how much money he got.

Even Dr. Elmer tried to horn in. He scratched the hole in his head and wheezed about how he'd love to have my father come speak, "If he has time in his busy schedule."

"He doesn't," I snapped, which brought a laugh from the class and made Elmer turn bright red.

All that week I did my best to be completely boring so I'd be left alone, and it worked. By Friday, no one bothered me about anything. I guess they figured the brilliant doctor had an idiot son, and that was fine with me. I thought the worst had passed, but the disaster came that next Monday.

It drizzled on Saturday, but by late Sunday night a hard rain was beating against the windows. The wind was howling and the limbs of the birch trees rubbed against the downspouts and batted the side of the house.

I don't know how late it was when I finally fell asleep, but when the alarm went off I was exhausted. I had to force myself to do everything. I couldn't find my shoes; I dropped my toothbrush in the toilet; I spilled my Wheaties on the floor. I was so late I had to run to the bus stop. Since it was still pouring, I was soaked by the time I got myself safely to the last seat in the back.

I wanted to sleep, so I scrunched myself into the corner and closed my eyes. The rumble of the bus was hypnotic. I had almost dozed off when I felt a hand on my shoulder. It was John.

"Have you seen this week's *Star-Enquirer?*" he asked.

I just stared at him. It was such an odd question, and he had such a strange look on his face, almost as if someone had died.

"You're not going to like what it says," he went on, "but you'll want to read it." He dropped the magazine on the seat next to me and walked back to his own seat.

The *Star-Enquirer* is one of those supermarket scandal sheets full of articles about Jackie's latest lover and messages from Elvis from the other side. It's not the kind of magazine I'd expected John to read. But when I looked down at it, one headline jumped out at me: **LASKER DOC A DEVIL!**

That woke me up. There was no index, but I found the article in a hurry.

A Tale of Two Fausts

In Germany, hundreds of years ago, a chilling legend grew about a brilliant doctor who sold his soul to the devil for power. That doctor's name was Faust. Today, in America, the scientific world has just given its highly prestigious Lasker Award to a Dr. Faust in Seattle. Just a coincidence? Maybe. But is it also just a coincidence that the work of this modern Dr. Faust has been condemned as evil and has even been called the work of the devil?

80

Hitler's Doctors!

To find out, we first called Dr. Paul Driscoll, editor of the journal *Science in Service of Christ*, and asked him for his evaluation of Dr. Faust's research. "The most important thing to understand," Dr. Driscoll told us, "is that these experiments started with Hitler. Hitler wanted to use genetics to further the development of his master race. His SS doctors performed unspeakable procedures, but failed. Dr. Faust is doing the same type of work in the same field, and he is succeeding. This work could lead to a world where some men are masters and others are slaves.

"I don't know why Dr. Faust chooses to do this type of research. I'm not saying that he is an evil man. I don't even know him."

A Stone Wall

Who does know this controversial prize-winner? We contacted all of America's leading scientists. None of them was able — or willing — to give us any details about the private life of Dr. Faust. Most failed to reply or to return our phone calls. And Dr. Faust himself? Despite repeated requests, he absolutely refused to speak with any representative of the *Star-Enquirer*.

But the questions raised by Dr. Driscoll were too disturbing to be ignored. And Dr. Faust's silence was too suspicious. Was he hiding something? We had to find out!

It was his son, seventeen-year-old Joe Faust, Jr., who in an exclusive interview revealed the dark side of the story. "My father has nothing to do with me," confessed young Joe. "I'm not smart enough for him. As far as he's concerned, if you're not a genius, you're nothing."

Dr. Faust forces his son to attend an all-white private school even though the boy repeatedly begged his father to let him attend a racially mixed public school right around the block. "My father acts like I'd catch a disease if I rubbed elbows with anything other than rich white kids," young Joe complained.

And what of Dr. Faust's wife? Here the story takes a bizarre turn. Young Joe revealed that his father encourages his wife to spend hours alone with boys half her age! And these young boys are naked!

It seems that Mrs. Faust, who calls herself an "artist," hires college boys to come to her house and take off their clothes while she "sculpts" them. Not surprisingly, no one is ever in the room while this "art" work goes on.

The Future of Our Country

We went back to Dr. Driscoll and presented him with this portrait of the household of the prizewinning Dr. Faust. "I can't say I'm

shocked. Racism, elitism, sexual perversity —
those are things that come when Science is cut
off from Religion, from values. It's frightening
to think that Dr. Faust has won America's
most prestigious scientific award. It's almost
like giving the award to Satan."

5

Shame. That's what I felt. Shame for what I had
said; shame for the humiliation the article would
bring my parents. I knew that not many professors
at the university or kids at a school like Eastside
rushed out and bought the *Star-Enquirer* hot off
the press, but I also knew that eventually a lot of
people would read that article.

I wandered through the school day like a zombie.
The week before I'd wanted to be alone and everyone was asking me questions. Now I wanted someone to come up and say something, but no one did.
It was like I had leprosy.

The morning classes went on forever. There was
a test in history. I'd studied and I did well on the
multiple choice, but I couldn't make myself concentrate on the essay questions. I left two of them
blank, so I knew I'd failed. In math we did problems
on the board. Anyati went on a rampage, but the
victim was the pimply kid and not me. In physics
everyone but me had a great time throwing bits of

clay around while Elmer yelled, "Get a tight seal on the tubing." Monbouquette had us read silently in French. That was better — I just opened the book and thought.

Then the lunch bell rang and I wandered out to the back stairwell to eat. A cold wind whipped across the playground and the sky was dark. I hunched my shoulders and started to bite into my salami sandwich when Ryan Blake and Mary Staraska came around the corner.

I knew them from English class mainly, though Blake was in my P.E. class, too. He was a total loser, one of those guys who can't even catch. It was perfect that he'd hook up with someone like Mary. She was tall and skinny and had pale skin and dark hair. She was also the closest anyone at Eastside came to being punk — black pants, black sweatshirt, lots of earrings. When she read out loud in English, she was always real dramatic. John told me that she'd played Antigone the year before in the school play.

They nodded and I nodded back. Then they sat down with their backs to me and started talking in hushed voices. After a few minutes they stood up and went underneath the stairwell where I couldn't see them. I figured they were going to do a little lunchtime necking back there, but it seemed they were having a ferocious argument. After a few minutes Mary shouted in a tormented voice: "Why this is hell, nor am I out of it!"

That scared me. I peeked around the corner, half expecting to see Ryan choking her to death. When they saw the expression on my face they both laughed. "Nothing's wrong," Ryan said. "We're in the Drama Club. We're rehearsing *Dr. Faustus*."

I returned to my step. For the next few minutes all I heard was Mary shouting about the power of Lucifer, the terror of damnation, and the torment of ten thousand hells.

I finished my lunch and hustled away.

"You playing today?" John asked when he saw me.

"If there's room."

"There's room. Take Doyle, OK?"

It was the first time I'd played on those courts. The rims were so tight that if you didn't swish your shots, they weren't going down. I didn't swish anything. But it wasn't just my shooting that was off, it was my whole game. Doyle beat me backdoor three times; I blew two fast breaks with bad passes; I even palmed the ball for no reason at all. If I did anything good, I don't remember it.

In English Miss Mitchell passed out copies of *Dr. Faustus*. It was a different book from the one I had at home. There were no pictures and the print was smaller. "Don't be discouraged by the language," she said as she wrote our assignment on the board. "You'll find it difficult for a few pages, but then you'll get the hang of it. You'll look back and wonder why you ever struggled."

We didn't read anything in class that day. Instead, we had a discussion on whether or not there was a devil. Mary Staraska said something about God creating man and man creating the devil. But then Marie Milligan raised her hand. "The devil is just a superstition," she said.

Nobody seemed to disagree with Marie except for Ryan Blake. "What about Hitler and Stalin?" he said. "You can't laugh them off as a superstition. It seems to me they're pretty strong evidence there must be a devil."

John answered that. "I think Hitler was insane. Stalin probably was, too. My uncle's a psychiatrist and he says that most criminal behavior is a sign of mental illness."

Miss Mitchell looked up at the clock. The bell was about to ring. "Fair enough, class. I guess the devil is out of fashion. But this semester I'd like all of you to try to imagine that you were born in the fifteen-hundreds and you believe, really believe, in the devil. It will help you understand the play."

That day at gym we played basketball for the first time. Raible used the old beauty contest method of choosing teams. John, Ray Snellinger, Alex Reynolds, and Seth Sharkey were captains. The rest of us lined up against the wall and prayed we wouldn't be the last one selected. John picked me first. As I stepped forward, I saw Alex and Ray exchange a glance of disbelief. Alex actually snickered. I can't say I blamed him. I hadn't shown anything in the lunch game, but I vowed to make him eat that grin.

I tried — I don't think I've ever tried harder — but nothing worked. My legs were heavy and slow. My shooting touch was way off. I couldn't come up with any loose balls. Players three inches shorter were outrebounding me. Reynolds snuffed the two shots I took in the lane. Basketball had always been the only thing I was really good at, but suddenly I was lousy at that, too.

"Don't worry about it," John said as we headed to the shower room. "Everybody has a bad game. We'll get them next time."

"Right," I said, "we'll crush them."

6

It was a long bus ride home. There had been another accident on the bridge, so we inched along for an hour. I sat alone in the back and rehearsed a dozen ways to explain to my parents what had happened. None of them was any good.

When the bus finally dropped me off, I had given up. I'd just let whatever was going to happen, happen. But I couldn't get myself to go into the house right away. The Mercedes wasn't in front, so my father was at work. There was no light in the studio upstairs, which meant my mother was waiting for me downstairs. I just stood on the lawn in the rain. My hair was plastered to my head and cold raindrops began to work their way down my back before I finally went up the porch steps and into the house.

I opened the front door more like a thief than a member of the family. I hung up my coat and took off my wet shoes, something I usually forget to do. Then I slipped into the living room, feeling like a worm.

My mother was sitting on the sofa drinking a glass of red wine. She looked calm. No one would have ever known there was anything wrong, except for two things. She was smoking a cigarette and the telephone had been disconnected and sat, the cord wrapped neatly around it, next to her on the sofa.

"Sit down, Joe," she murmured. "Sit down and tell me about it."

I sat and I talked. I told her about coming home and seeing all those cars in front of the house. I told her how this woman called out to me, and how we walked together to Sunset Hill Park, and how she asked about the family.

"And then you told a complete stranger, a reporter, those things about me and your father?" she asked.

"Not exactly."

"What does that mean?"

"I said some of those things, but she twisted them."

"How did she twist them?"

"It's hard to explain."

"Try."

I didn't say anything. I couldn't. My mother stared at me. She stared at me as if I were a lump of clay or a piece of stone she were sizing up for the first time, wondering what use it could be put to. I couldn't stand that look. I excused myself and retreated to my room.

Once in my room I stood before the mirror and sized myself up. I had all the advantages. I was reasonably intelligent, not bad looking, and athletic. My parents cared about me, spent both time and money on me. And what had I done?

My grades were sinking; I had no friends; and I probably couldn't even make the basketball team. I was a total flop. And to top it off, I was a traitor.

I emptied out my book bag on the bed and lay down. I had homework in every class. I began with English.

In the summer when I'd skimmed through the opening pages of *Dr. Faustus,* I hadn't worried if I didn't understand something. Reading for a class was entirely different. I must have gone over that first scene four times before I followed it.

Faustus has solved every problem, met every challenge. But there's one thing he doesn't have, can never have: unlimited power. He decides that since God made the world the way it is, God must want man to be unhappy. So Faustus turns his back on God and sells his soul to the devil for twenty-four years of power.

Turning to the devil sounds crazy, but a part of me admired him for stepping over the edge, for breaking through the boundaries. For seventeen years my parents and my teachers had been telling me to do the right thing, to do this and that. And most of the time I'd done it, or at least tried to. And where had it gotten me? I didn't know what anything added up to. Faustus had the guts to try to find some answers, even if it meant going a different way. That couldn't be all bad.

I'd been reading about an hour when my father came home. I heard him talking to my mother in the living room. Then I heard his footsteps on the stairs. I wouldn't have blamed him if he had barged right in and started screaming at me, but he knocked before he came in.

He sat on the chair across from my bed, lit a cigarette, and gazed out the window. "This is a beautiful city, isn't it?" he said.

I nodded, then I took a deep breath. "I don't know what happened to me. I don't know why I told her that stuff. And the way she wrote it was all different from what I meant."

He took a drag on his cigarette. "Did you know that she worked for the *Star-Enquirer*?"

"No, she didn't tell me who she worked for and I didn't think to ask. She didn't even take notes.

I figured she was only talking to me because she couldn't get to you and Mom right then. I never thought —"

He held up his hand and stopped me. "It's OK, Joe. There's no point in stewing over it. What's been said can't be taken back. It's going to be difficult for all of us for the next few months, but it will blow over. Now wash up; we'll go out for pizza."

7

The next morning at breakfast my father told me he wanted me to stay home from school. "You need a break and so do I. We'll both take the day off. I'd like to show you around the labs, have you meet some of my new colleagues. We could eat lunch and then play some racquetball at the Faculty Club. How does that sound?"

I was stunned. The last thing I wanted to do was to meet new people. All I wanted to do was hide. And I'd assumed my father would want me to hide. I wouldn't have blamed him if he locked me in my room, or down in the basement, or out of the house, for that matter.

"Don't you think it'd be better to wait a little while?" I asked.

My father shook his head. "No, I'd like to do it today, OK?"

The Genetics building is on the Montlake Cut, overlooking Lake Washington.

"That's a great view," I said as my father sat behind his desk writing something in a notebook.

He stopped and stared out the window. "You know, Joe, sometimes in the afternoon I look at the traffic on the bridge and wonder which one of the buses you're on, who you're talking to, what you're talking about."

"Really?"

"Yes, I do. Quite often, actually." He stood up. "Well, shall we go to the labs?"

For the next two hours we walked in and out of shiny white rooms. I looked through at least a dozen microscopes and nodded my head and pretended I understood something of what I was seeing. I met research assistants, janitors, associate professors, secretaries, graduate students, and deans. "This is my son, Joe," my father said every time he introduced me. I shook more than two dozen hands and looked into more than two dozen faces. It was tough for me, and I'm sure it was tough for my father. I could feel people thinking: "So this is the little weasel who dragged his parents through the garbage." I knew my father could feel it, too.

We ate lunch at the Health Sciences cafeteria. It was loud. Trays clattered, silverware dropped. It wasn't much different from Eastside's cafeteria, except for the smoking.

"What do you think of the department?" my father asked.

"It's great. It must be wonderful to work here."

He pushed his chair back and lit a cigarette. "I've always been happy in a laboratory. I still remember determining the sex of fruit flies as a sophomore." He smiled. "I spent hours after school in that lab."

"We did the same experiment at Emerson," I said. "My colony of all males quadrupled overnight."

My father laughed. "Is that true? You never told me that story before."

"That's why I got that B minus in Biology."

"I would have helped you, Joe. You should have asked."

"I wanted to do it myself."

He stubbed out his cigarette, folded his hands on the table, and looked me in the eye. "I'm your father, Joe. It's only natural that I'd want to help you. That's not wrong, is it? I want you to learn as much as you can so that you can go as far as your talents will take you. That's why I wanted Eastside; that's why I'd like to see you at Stanford. I want what's best for you."

He paused. I guess he was expecting me to say something. But there was nothing I could say.

He loosened his tie. "That's also why I don't understand how you could have said those things to the *Star-Enquirer*. Tell me what I've done that's so awful. I go over it and over it, and I just don't understand what I've done wrong. It's obvious you resent me, you resent the things I'm trying to do for you. But tell me, please, why?"

This was my chance. I wanted to tell him right then, but I couldn't. I wanted to say to him: *I'm not as smart as you are and there's no point in pretending I ever will be. I'll never make any great scientific discovery. I'll never even be a scientist. I don't belong at Stanford. I'm not the son you want.*

"You've got it wrong, Dad. I appreciate all you've done for me. I really do. It's just that some-times . . ."

I stopped. Nothing I could ever say would do any good. I could see it in his face. When we finished lunch, he never mentioned racquetball. Instead, he drove me home. As I got out of the car, he told me he'd be back late that night. "I've got work to catch up on. Make sure you tell your mother."

"I will."

My mother was lost in her own work upstairs. I went to my room and spent the afternoon reading the scene that comes right after Dr. Faustus sells his soul. You'd think Faustus would be frightened by what he'd done, but it's almost like he's drunk with his new power — that's how happy he is. The whole world is exciting for him again. I wondered if any-thing would ever make the world look that good to me.

8

Those were rough weeks. We got a new, unlisted number and plugged the telephone back in. But one Saturday members of some sect of Christian fundamentalists spent the afternoon marching around in front of our house, and TV crews were there to film them. And after the fundamentalists were gone, a free-lance photographer camped out on our lawn hoping to get a picture of my mother with one of her male models. My father had to chase him off. Finally there were a couple of days when nothing happened. "It's blown over," my mother said. "Nobody is interested anymore." But it didn't blow over; it got weird. When I went out one Monday morning, there were rocks all over the front porch. I swept them back into the flower bed and forgot about it. Two days later the welcome mat disappeared. The next day the fuchsia basket was smashed, and on Sunday an azalea bush was uprooted and thrown in the street.

My mother called the police.

They came to the house that evening after dinner. They sat at the kitchen table and scribbled down a few facts. Then the older cop asked my father if he was the professor who'd won the award. My father nodded. Then the policeman pointed at me. "That means you're the son." I looked away. "Well, Dr. Faust, I don't know if we'll ever catch the nitwit who's doing this stuff, but I do know this: Sonny-boy's big mouth is the cause. You wouldn't believe the number of people who read those magazines. I bet there are ten thousand people in Seattle who think you're the devil himself."

After the police car sped off, my mother switched off the porch light and we all sat silently in the front room. The clock on the mantel ticked away the minutes. Then an inspiration came to me.

"Why can't I call a press conference and take back what I said? I'm not afraid. I'll admit that I was a stupid fool and a liar and then everyone will leave us alone."

It was such an obvious solution I couldn't understand why I hadn't thought of it before. I not only wasn't afraid of telling the world what an idiot I'd been, I positively wanted to do it. It would make amends, make it clear how wrong I was, make me feel less guilty.

I sat on the edge of my chair, ecstatic with the beauty of my plan. I couldn't understand why neither my mother nor my father jumped up and patted me on the back and told me they had been waiting for me to make that kind of offer. But they didn't budge.

"Joe, it's nice of you, but it wouldn't work," my mother finally said.

"Why wouldn't it work?"

"Because everyone will think we forced you to do it. People like to think the worst. It would start the whole thing up again."

"So what can I do?"

"These people are trying to make us crack," my father said. "The best thing we can do is to hold together."

9

That week Raible brought out brand-new leather basketballs in P.E. "You guys can break these in," he said as he tossed them onto the court. "Tryouts are coming up."

The second I picked one up I felt a surge of confidence. There's nothing like the feel of a new leather ball with deep seams. With a ball like that, you can get just the right backspin to make your shots lay on the rims instead of bounding off. You don't get the good rolls with a cheap ball that has worn-out seams.

I was ready to burn up the court that day. The first time down, I fed John underneath on a post-up. The defense collapsed on him, so he kicked the ball back out to me. It wasn't a hard pass, just the right amount of zip. I squared up for the soft jumper. I knew if I hit the first one everything would fall in place. But somehow, in a way I don't understand, the ball went through my hands and out of bounds. And it didn't happen just once, it happened three more times in that game. It got so the guys didn't want to pass to me.

When gym ended, I stood at center court and stared at the basket. For the first time in my life it looked strange to me. I felt I didn't belong on a basketball court anymore. I was afraid it was more than a slump. You come out of slumps. I was afraid I had lost it.

And it wasn't just at P.E. that I'd lost it. I'd been letting all of my classes slide, even English. After we'd taken the test on the first half of *Dr. Faustus,* so many kids complained about how hard it was to understand that Miss Mitchell had switched back to our anthology of short stories and poems. Everyone else was happier for those three weeks, but that stuff didn't interest me.

The day after my fiasco with the new basketballs Miss Mitchell came in, sat down on top of her desk, and told us to put our anthology away. "We're going to finish *Dr. Faustus* during the next few weeks," she said, and the class groaned. Then she held up her hand to quiet us. "I know most of you haven't enjoyed it so far. That's why today I want to try something different. We're not going to discuss any speeches or read any scenes out loud. All I want you to do is to tell me what would tempt you to sell your soul. I know all of you can do that."

Eddie Doyle whispered to John that he'd sell his soul to get out of finishing the play. The kids around him laughed, and Miss Mitchell called on him. "Eddie, share your joke."

"It was stupid."

"Come on, Eddie, don't leave the rest of us out."

So Eddie told his joke again. Miss Mitchell smiled. "No such luck," she said. "Any other ideas?"

One of the football players talked about a full scholarship to UCLA followed by a million-dollar contract with the 49ers. John mentioned immortality. Sandy Perry pointed out that immortality was no good unless you don't age. "I'd like to be eighteen forever." After that everybody started laughing and having a good time imagining what they could get in return for their souls. One guy said he'd give anything for an hour in a hot tub with Miss September.

"OK," Miss Mitchell said once we finished laughing. "Now let's look at this from the other side. What does Faustus lose when he sells his soul?"

Nobody said anything for a while, then John raised his hand. "If you believe in heaven, then he loses that."

"But does Faustus believe in heaven?" Miss Mitchell caught my eye. "Joe, what do you think?"

I remembered how good the world looked to Faustus after he'd struck his bargain with the devil. "I don't think he believes in heaven or hell. He knows he's got one life and he wants to get the most out of it that he can. What's a soul, anyway? You can't see it or feel it. If you lost it, how would you ever know it was gone? Faustus is smart to sell it for power."

Mary Staraska raised her hand. "Just because you can't see something doesn't mean it's not there," she said. "We aren't machines. We have feelings and emotions. Those things have to come from somewhere, don't they?"

The class was silent for a moment. Then Eddie Doyle raised his hand. "I don't know about feelings and emotions and all that, but I do think you'd have to be an idiot to sell your soul. The odds are probably ten to one against there being a hell. But if that one chance comes through, you'd spend several zillion years frying. What could be worth taking that kind of risk?"

I kept quiet like everybody else, but I had the answer to that question, too. Everything had gone wrong for so long that I wanted one thing to go right. It might have seemed trivial to somebody else, and maybe it was, but what I wanted to go right was basketball. I wanted to hit a twenty-foot jumper from the corner in a tie game with the clock ticking down to zero and the crowd on its feet and out of its mind. I wanted packed gyms to chant my name; I wanted opponents to shake their heads in awe; I wanted my teammates to look up to me in wonder. I wanted one full season of glory. I didn't care if it were only temporary, if it would all be forgotten by April. At least I'd have known greatness one time in my life. That would have been worth it.

The bell rang. Once I was outside of class I couldn't believe how worked up I'd gotten. The devil wasn't going to pop out of the fireplace and offer me a great hook shot for my immortal soul. The whole thing was total nonsense.

When I got home that afternoon, my mother met me at the door. "Your father's upstairs sleeping," she said.

"Sleeping? In the middle of the afternoon?"

She nodded. "At work he came down with a migraine headache, a bad one. So no stereo, OK?"

10

During the next three weeks he had four more attacks. Each one seemed to age him a little. The bags under his eyes grew darker; the lines across his forehead became deeper. The skin around his jaw sagged.

It was around then I started killing the late afternoons walking around. I wasn't going anywhere or doing anything; I just was sick of sitting in my room.

Sometimes I'd walk through old Ballard, past all the taverns and the cheap hotels. If it rained, I'd go down Market Street and cut over to the railroad tracks that lead to the Chittenden Locks. I spent hours huddled underground staring at the salmon through the plate-glass window.

Once, when it was sunny, I crossed the footbridge to Magnolia and hiked all the way to the Fishermen's Terminal. I watched some men as they unloaded their equipment and cleaned their boat.

"Watch your head!" one of them shouted, and his buddy jumped clear of a crab pot that would have brained him. A second later they were both working again. It was a close call, but they didn't seem to give it a thought. All I did was think.

One day I passed an old deserted building not too far from my house, maybe a mile at the most. The doors and windows were boarded up, but I could still make out the words "Ballard Boys and Girls Club" underneath the graffiti.

I didn't pay much attention to it the first time, but for the next few days I kept returning to that building. Something drew me to it. Not that it was anything to look at. The brown-and-white paint was peeling off the wood siding, but even in its prime it must have been ugly. It wasn't until Friday that it hit me: there had to be a gym in there.

I'd never broken into a building before, and I couldn't believe how easy it was. It took one hard tug on a board over a window in the back and the nails gave a sickening creak. I was certain the whole world heard it, so I ducked behind the nearest bush and waited, my heart pounding. Nothing happened. A crow cawed; a car drove by; a light rain started to fall. I crept back out, gave the board another tug, and it came completely out of the window frame. I laid it carefully, silently, on the ground and scrambled inside.

I found myself in what must have been the lobby. Across from me was a big desk and an empty trophy case. A Ping-Pong table had been folded up and pushed against the wall to my right. On the left were two old pinball machines, and the sign above the door across the lobby read "Richard Roth Gymnasium."

I swung the double doors open and went inside. The place was perfect — wooden floor, sturdy rims, full-size backboards. Sure it was dirty, dark, and more than a little damp and smelly. The important thing was that it was mine. I could work on my game alone.

11

Saturday morning I snuck back to the gym. At first I was worried someone would hear the ball bouncing, but after about five minutes I gave up stewing about it. The building was off the street; cars were driving by all day. I would take my chances.

I was going to work strictly on my shot. My mechanics had gone completely off, so I started with the basics, square one. I made myself get the ball up into my fingertips, made myself concentrate on a good follow-through with the wrist, made myself put a little backspin on the ball. I worked around the key, mostly taking fifteen-footers. Little by little the touch returned. After an hour I was dropping in rainbows from everywhere.

That's when I let my imagination go. I'm embarrassed to admit it, but I played these pretend games where I was Joe Faust, Boston Celtic. I burned Michael Jordan on a slashing drive to the hoop; I pump-faked Isiah Thomas into a foul that gave me a three-point play; I snuck inside Charles Barkley for a tip-in at the buzzer. In two hours I played a season and had a career's worth of highlights. I was unstoppable.

12

On Monday at school all I could think about was basketball. I'd shot so well in that old gym that I couldn't wait to play. But around ten o'clock the rain started. It was light at first, but grew heavier and heavier. There would be no basketball game at lunch. It didn't matter, though, there was still P.E. My slump was history — I could feel it. I was on my way up!

But gym began differently that day. After we did our warm-ups, Raible asked everyone who was trying out for the basketball team to step forward. There were seven of us. Raible paced back and forth, looking us over. Then he told me and two other guys to follow him to his office. The rest of the class, including John and the other varsity players, went off to start the games.

"I just wanted you boys to know where you stand," Raible said when we were alone with him. "We've got a good team coming back, an excellent team. There are four seniors who lettered, four juniors who played some varsity last year, and our freshman team was undefeated. That's why you'll start with Mr. Schmidt on the junior varsity. Schmidt's a good guy and he knows basketball. If I've made a mistake, he'll tell me. But junior varsity isn't the end of the world. You'll have fun and you'll get to play."

I'd seen Schmidt teaching freshman P.E. He always wore hard shoes. He wanted the class to shoot two-hand set shots and toss up free throws between their legs like Rick Barry. My father knew more about basketball than Mr. Schmidt. I shuffled back onto the court.

Raible came over to watch my game. I had to show him, right then, that I was varsity material. Seth Sharkey was guarding me. I gave him a stutter-step dribble and took the ball baseline, fifteen feet out. Swish! The next time down I buried a jumper from just inside the top of the key. After that, Sharkey went for a pump fake and I drove by him and hit a jumper in the lane over Snellinger. Three trips, three baskets, three meals of dirt for Sharkey!

And three meals of dirt for Raible. As I back-pedaled I looked over at him, gloating. It was a stupid, bush thing to do. Sharkey was a player. He saw my eyes shift and instantly blew right by me for an easy hoop. As the ball went through, Raible turned his back and headed over to watch the game on the other court.

In the locker room John asked me if I'd been given the JV speech.

"You got it. I've been cut and I haven't even tried out."

"When I was a sophomore, Raible gave me that speech. But I played well and Schmidt moved me up. By the end of the year I was starting. If you can get your game in shape, you'll be all right."

I nodded. But I didn't believe it. I kept reliving that moment when Sharkey burned me. Maybe Raible had me pegged. Maybe I was strictly JV.

After school I went straight to my gym. I had to do more than get my game in shape; I had to make it perfect. I stretched for ten minutes, shot a few lay-ins, threw some crisp passes against the wall. I worked on rebounding by keeping the ball alive off the backboard. I jumped so many times that my calves ached. Next, I ran wind sprints for twenty minutes; and then I practiced stopping fast breaks. I backpedaled, head up, looking for an imaginary downcourt pass. I ran backward so fast that I fell again and again. But I didn't slow down, not once. I just got up and made myself go all out while still trying to keep my balance.

It wasn't until after I'd worked for two hours that I allowed myself a little stardom. Raible watched, clipboard in hand, as Seth Sharkey and I went one-on-one. Sharkey was tough, but I guarded him like a hawk. I stuffed his jumpers; I muscled him on the boards; I stripped him with my fast hands. On offense, I posted him down low and banked in soft, turnaround jumpers. I beat him 11–4, 11–6, 11–3. Raible blew the whistle. "Sharkey, maybe you'd be better off on junior varsity this year. You'll get to play more, and Mr. Schmidt's quite a guy."

13

That Friday was Halloween. When I got off the bus, I didn't go to my secret gym. It was the first day I'd missed in weeks. I was just too tired. I hadn't been sleeping well, and I was killing myself in P.E. in the basketball games. My shots were dropping and my defense was solid, but it always seemed like Raible was watching the other game when I did something good. If I screwed up, though, his eyes would be glued on me.

My father worked late that night. "Since it's just going to be the two of us," my mother said, "why don't you call Godfather's and have a pizza delivered?"

"Pepperoni OK with you?"

"That's fine."

After we finished the pizza and I'd washed the

dishes, I volunteered to pass out candy to the trick-or-treaters.

"Great," my mother said. "I've got a ton of work waiting for me in my studio. I don't know if many kids will come or not, but there are two bags of candy in the cabinet above the stove."

The doorbell rang for the first time just after six. I opened the door and saw a devil with horns and a pitchfork. "Boo!" he cried out. I jumped back in terror and he laughed and laughed.

About thirty little ghosts and goblins came, their parents waiting at the sidewalk. They went through one bag of Baby Ruths and half a bag of Butterfingers.

The last kids rang the doorbell around eight. My mother came down ten minutes later. She turned off the porch light and asked me how it went. "It was fun," I said, and then I climbed up to my room. Around ten-thirty my father came home so I flicked the stereo off.

I wasn't tired, so I curled up under an afghan by the window and read the assigned pages in *Dr. Faustus*. I'd reached the part that describes how Faustus uses the devil's power. He has Helen of Troy dance for him, he gets fancy grapes from India, and he plays practical jokes on people like the Pope — stupid stuff like that. I guess having power wasn't the whole story. You had to know what you wanted to do with it.

The night was so still and the hour was so late

that I noticed the car right away, especially when it stopped in front of the house.

Faustus, thou art damned! Those were the last words I read that night, and the way things worked out they could have applied to me. I heard car doors open and close, then low voices and an angry "Shut up!" I put the book down, switched off the light, and looked out.

Four guys stood on the lawn in front of our house. They had a large, flimsy wooden cross, which they were hammering into the grass. I could hear each dull thud as the wood penetrated the soft earth. I'm sure it took only a minute or two, but it seemed like they hammered for hours.

What I don't understand is why I didn't open the window and yell at them. They would have run to their car and driven off, and that would have been the end of it. It would have been just another botched Halloween prank. But I didn't yell. I watched.

The cross wobbled, but it stuck in the ground. One of them doused it with gasoline, lit a match, and the cross burst into flames with a *whoosh*. The light was so bright, so stunning, that I could see them stepping back, gasping at the fire.

They stood transfixed for a few moments. The tallest one picked up a rock and hurled it through our picture window. Then they were off and running, back to the red car. The doors slammed shut, the engine started, and they were down the block, around the corner, and gone. I knew I'd never forget that moment, though, because as they'd stood in the light of the blaze, I'd seen something I would have given anything not to see: I had seen Ross.

My father met the policemen on the lawn about ten minutes later. His face was ashen and he kept running his hands through his hair. My mother sat in the kitchen smoking and drinking coffee.

They were the same policemen, and they asked the same kinds of questions in the same dull voices. I sat on a chair in the corner. I hadn't told my parents what I had seen. The breaking glass had awakened them. My father had turned the garden hose on the cross, which had fallen forward and come within a few feet of the porch.

"Those goddamned maniacs!" he kept repeating. "They could have burned down the house with us in it!"

The police tried to be helpful, but it was clear they felt it was hopeless. They looked uncomfortable on the sofa. Their nightsticks were jammed against the cushions; their walkie-talkies blared strange static messages every few minutes. As they stood up to leave, the gray-haired one looked at me. "You didn't happen to see anything, did you?"

My throat went dry and I could feel my neck and ears turn bright red. I took a deep breath. "I saw it all. I heard the car pull up and I went to the window and watched them pound the cross in and light it on fire." My parents stared at me. The policemen sat down again. "There were four of them,"

I said, "but I recognized only one." I looked my father in the eye. "It was Ross."

"Ross!" my father shouted.

The gray-haired officer took me to the kitchen and peppered me with questions. Was I sure it was Ross? What was Ross's last name? Did I know his address? Did I know the names of any of the others? Had I seen any of them before? Did I think I'd be able to identify them if I saw them again?

He put his pen back in his shirt pocket. "This will do for tonight."

"What are you going to do now?" my father asked.

"Now we go to bed. We'll bring Ross in tomorrow. It's my guess he's responsible for all the damage you've had. If you're lucky, the court will make him pay, but don't count on it."

They said goodnight and shuffled out the door.

"It's been a long evening," my father said when they were gone. "I think we should try to get some sleep."

I nodded and went right to my room. But I couldn't sleep. I had to figure out why Ross had done it. What was he getting back at me for? Did he feel I'd betrayed him? Maybe it seemed to him that all summer I'd pretended to be different from the other Sunset Hill kids only to disappear into my fancy private school when September rolled around.

That made some sense, but not much. What Ross had done was out of all proportion. It was no joke, and there was no way he could have thought it was. All at once I hated him. He was dangerous, malicious, violent. It felt good to hate him. It made everything clear as glass, and simple.

But I couldn't hold that hate for long. I kept thinking about all the times I'd gone along with him when I knew what he was doing was wrong, all the times when if I'd acted just a little differently, he might have acted differently, too. Suddenly I felt everything was really my fault. It was a feeling I couldn't shake.

14

I've never been as tired as I was the next day. My mother said I could stay home. But I didn't want to look out the window and relive the whole thing all day, so I trudged off to the bus. For once, it was bright and sunny. If ever I wanted a gray, rainy day it was then.

I shuffled through my morning classes. I couldn't eat, and I didn't have any desire to play basketball, so at noon I went out to the field behind the gym and lay down on the grass. The blue sky was dotted with white clouds that looked like huge balls of cotton candy. It would be warm and then a cloud would cover the sun and it would go cold. I could hear guys playing football, dribbling basketballs, laughing, and shouting. Pretty soon the human sounds got all mixed up with the chirping of the birds and the dull roar of the distant cars. It flowed together, outside of me, and it was strangely pleasant.

I don't know how long I lay there, or what brought me to, but it wasn't the school bell. That had obviously rung a lot earlier.

I snuck into the main building, crept to my locker, and took out my English books.

Miss Mitchell didn't look happy when I slipped into the classroom, but she didn't give me a bad time the way most teachers would have. I found an empty seat in the back.

"Why do you think Faustus asks for exactly twenty-four years of power?"

The only hand that went up was Ryan Blake's. "Maybe he picked twenty-four years because that's the number of hours in a day," Ryan said. "Also it's a number that comes to mind right away."

"It doesn't come to my mind," Eddie Doyle whispered, and the rest of the class snickered. I could tell Miss Mitchell was frustrated. I raised my hand and she nodded at me.

"I can see Ryan's point. One day is a complete thing. It has a beginning, a middle, and an ending. Faustus wants power for a complete cycle, and twenty-four years would cover the rest of his adult life. Maybe he wanted to have that feeling of completion."

"That's a very perceptive comment," Miss Mitchell said. "It shows you've given this play some thought."

I wish the day had ended right there, but I still had gym class. I played ugly. Sharkey stripped me time after time. I was short with my shots and my defense was atrocious. I didn't hustle after loose balls or take off on the fast break. I was so bad that John asked me if I was sick.

Raible finally blew the whistle to end class. "Listen up!" he shouted. "If you're interested in varsity or junior varsity basketball, come to my office now and pick up your registration packet."

Raible had stared right at me when he'd said "junior varsity." The way I'd played, I didn't blame him. But I couldn't bear the idea of spending my senior year on a JV team coached by a guy who wore hard shoes and wanted everyone to shoot free throws toilet-style. I didn't pick up the packet.

When I stepped off the bus that day, I went straight to my gym. I stretched out, then practiced. I dribbled up and down the court, left-handed, right-handed, switch-over, between the legs, behind the back. Then I worked on the jumper, and not just from my favorite spots. After that I did running hooks and twisting lay-ins. I finished with twenty push-ups and sixty sit-ups. I worked so hard I was dead on my feet, and then I worked some more.

Late that night it started to rain. First there were

just a few drops on the glass, and then the whole window was streaked. The rain was peaceful and so was the darkness. I liked looking out into it. Somehow the blackness was soothing. As bad as things were, one thought consoled me: at least everything was over.

But that's when it really began.

PART
THREE

1

It was November 16 — a foggy morning had turned into a cold, gray day. Winter was coming. When I stole into the gym after school, I realized my hideaway wasn't going to do me much good for much longer. The problem was simple — every day more darkness was creeping in.

It depressed me because I had actually been getting used to my routine. I would sleepwalk through the morning classes at school, then come back to life for English and P.E. in the afternoon. The bus ride was long and boring, but it would end in the secret gym where I played my magical, imaginary games. I'd arrive home late, eat a quick dinner, and then disappear into my room to study, listen to records, and sleep. It wasn't a great life, but it wasn't bad.

With the onset of winter, I was stuck shooting

baskets in the dim light cast by a distant street lamp. The gym was so dark it was even hard to run. And the place was starting to creep me out. That little bit of light from outside caused the backboard and the hoop to cast a weird shadow on the side wall.

It was that shadow that set me off. I had never noticed it before, though it must have been there all the time. The real backboard and hoop were completely normal. But the shadow backboard was distorted, cracked down the middle, one half a foot higher than the other. The shadow of the hoop was huge. I remember thinking how easy it would be to make baskets if a real hoop were like that.

As I stared at the shadow and then at the solid hoop, it struck me that they were both real. You couldn't touch the shadow, but that didn't make it any less real. The solid hoop and the shadow hoop were just two forms of the same thing.

That's what Miss Mitchell had been trying to tell us about *Dr. Faustus*. Faustus, she said, broke through the physical world into the shadow world, the spiritual world. It had always seemed like hocus-pocus in the classroom, but there it was before me. A circular iron rim, a rectangular wooden backboard. And on the wall its fantastic double: a huge hoop oddly mounted on a split backboard.

I bounced the basketball once. I heard the familiar thud as it hit the floor. Then, as I caught the ball, I heard the echo. It was the same thing all over again. The physical world, the thud of the basketball against the floor; and the spiritual world, the echo.

My heart was racing. I heard a clap of thunder and raindrops pounded on the metal roof. The gym grew darker and a strange, almost malignant mist seemed to fill it. Then an eerie thought came to me: the mist somehow held the devil. I felt something around me. I didn't want to fall under its spell, so I dribbled once and took a jump shot from beyond the top of the key. The sound was unmistakable: Swish!

The shot was so perfect that the spin on the ball carried it right back into my hands. I shot again, swished it again, and back the ball came. A third time I did it, then a fourth. I knew it wasn't just me shooting, that it couldn't be just me. A fifth and a sixth time I hit perfect shots and each time the spin on the ball brought it back. With each shot the mist thickened, the light grew dimmer. When the seventh shot whistled through, I knew the devil was tempting me. He was showing me the power of his world.

On the eighth jump shot I didn't even try. I let the ball go with just the easiest flick of the wrist: Swish! I shot again and number nine tickled the twine and came back as if I had it on a string. It was an incredible feeling, to be able to do it all so effortlessly. I had to keep on being able to do it. I think that's why I made the vow.

"Give me a full season, give me twenty-four games of this power, and my soul is yours."

I faced the basket, took a deep breath, and let the last jump shot go.

Inside the gym all motion slowed. Up the ball went in a high arc. It seemed to stop and rest for a moment at the top, and only then did it hurtle down with a terrifying beauty. It was the perfect shot, the final swish, and as it whistled through the net I couldn't help wondering if my soul had plunged into the devil's camp for all eternity.

2

When I crawled out the window and was back on the street, none of it seemed possible. The world was too normal. Men and women were coming home from work, kids from school. They were picking up newspapers off lawns, pulling letters out of crammed mailboxes. It was crazy to think I'd sold my soul to the devil. Things like that only happened in books. It was impossible. But then those ten perfect jump shots in the near dark were hardly possible either.

The rain had let up, but the sky was dark. I cut through an alley and tried to hustle home before there was another downpour. When I was about twenty-five yards up the alley, a bunch of thugs came around the corner. One was riding a Kawasaki 750 and the others were smoking, laughing, and punching one another.

I crossed to the opposite side of the alley, doing my best not to make eye contact, but as I stepped around a tipped-over garbage can, one of the guys pointed at me. About thirty seconds later, the motorcycle accelerated straight toward me. I didn't flinch, though. I walked straight and tall and the biker had to veer off.

I'd hoped that this little razzing was all that was in store for me, but no such luck. The other three guys cut across the alley to intercept me and the motorcycle doubled back and closed off any retreat. I was surrounded.

"You're the guy who ratted on Ross, aren't you?" the biggest kid sneered. He had tattoos on his arm and acne scars on his face.

"Yeah, I guess I am."

"Pretty tough guy with the cops around."

"You're pretty tough yourself with all your buddies around," I shot right back. "I'm just wondering if you'd have had the guts to say anything to me if you were alone."

I couldn't believe what I was saying. I've always been a coward and this hood looked like he thrived on street fights. But once I'd started, a strange power took hold of me. It was that power, wherever it came from, that was talking.

I think the tone of my voice surprised even the bruiser. He just stood still, chomping on his gum.

Then something clicked in his thick skull. When he looked to his left, I knew in a flash what was coming.

It was as if everything were in slow motion. A big roundhouse right was looping toward my head. I ducked it easily and came in with a straight right of my own into his soft gut. He doubled over. A second later one of his cronies threw a punch. I tucked my head down so that it just grazed me. Then I flat-out decked him with a left hook. I spun around and gave the motorcyclist a hard push. The Kawasaki toppled over and pinned him down. There was just one guy left, and he held up his hands and backed away.

Right then an old geezer came out of his house yelling that he was going to call the police. "You stop that *vighting!*" he screamed, his face red with anger. "Stop *vighting!*"

The four guys stared at me, then at him, and took off.

That night my left hand started to swell up. It hurt so badly I couldn't hold a knife at dinner. I thought it might be broken, so I had to tell my father I had been in a fight.

"What was it about?" he asked.

"Just public school—private school stuff. It happens all the time, only usually you don't have to throw any punches."

"But four against one doesn't happen all the time," he insisted. "I think I'll call the principal over there."

"Dad, just forget it, OK? Nyra Jefferson's not going to do anything. Let's just go to the hospital and get it X-rayed."

It wasn't broken, but I did end up with a fever and had to miss two days of school. I spent most of that time trying to make sense of what had happened. I wasn't a fighter, never had been. Yet somehow I had taken out those hoods. There was no explanation, or at least no explanation that wasn't crazy.

3

It was Friday when I headed back to school. My fingers still hurt, but my temperature was normal and I was sick of staying home after two days of sitting inside soaking my hand. The cold morning rain felt good and the noise on the bus sounded like music.

John said hello when I plopped myself on the seat next to him. He asked me why I had been out and I told him I'd slammed the car door on my hand. I held up my swollen knuckles.

"Those are ugly," he said. "Do you think you can still play ball?"

I opened my left hand and stretched the fingers out. Then I rotated the wrist.

"I can play," I said, wondering what was up.

"I guess you didn't hear what happened to Sharkey," John said.

"No, I didn't."

"At the tail end of practice Tuesday he came down on Snellinger's foot. Sharkey's ankle twisted completely under. I talked to him last night. He said it's swollen and blue from his toes to his calf. The doctor told him he'd have been better off to have broken it. He'll miss the whole season."

"That's a tough break. He was a solid point guard."

"Yeah, Sharkey's good." John paused. "But in the summer — when you were on your game — you were just as good."

I flushed red. "I don't know about that." I wanted to believe him, but it had been a long time since I'd been on my game.

"You were, Joe. Really."

We sat silently for a moment. I know I was thinking about the warm summer air and the games with Ross, and I figured John was, too.

John spoke first. "Anyway, Sharkey's injury really screws up the team. Raible spent about thirty minutes watching the JV practice, but he didn't bring anybody up. He wants those sophomores to play; he doesn't want them on the varsity sitting on the bench. He has to do something, though. We've only got three guards now. Practice was a mess."

John didn't say it, but we were both thinking the same thing. If I'd just swallowed my pride and worked out with the junior varsity, that fourth guard would have been me.

At P.E. that day Raible watched my game. My hand hurt, but I couldn't let it bother me. The first time down I took a bounce pass from Burns and hit a twenty-footer. John got me the ball in the corner two more times and I buried both of them. The third time we worked that play Doyle jumped out on me. I drove by him, John's man picked me up, and I dished back to John for a lay-in.

That's how the whole game went. I was handling the ball well, sinking my outside shots, and running the court like a demon. I wanted to play forever.

When class ended, I was covered with sweat.

Raible intercepted me on my way to the locker room.

"Faust, if you've got a minute I'd like to talk to you."

I followed him into his little cubicle. He sat down, folded his hands in front of him on his desk, and stared at me. "Joe, I won't mince words. You've been playing better recently, and today you put together some solid minutes."

"Thanks, Coach."

He tapped his pen on the desk. "You must have heard what happened to Sharkey."

I nodded.

"We're short a guard now. I could bring up one of the sophomores from the junior varsity, but neither of them is ready. Frankly, I'd like to give you a chance. I guess just about everybody knows you've had your problems. You should have worked out with the JV's, but you're a senior, and I know that's tough on the ego."

"I wish I had, Coach. I don't know why I didn't. I miss playing on a team. I miss it a lot."

He opened his drawer and pulled out a large envelope and handed it to me. "That's what I wanted to hear. As soon as you get all those forms filled out, you can come to practice. I don't guarantee anything. I might end up moving you down to junior varsity and bringing up one of the sophomores. Even if you stick, you might not play a minute the entire year."

"You won't hear any complaints from me, Coach."

"Good. That's the right attitude." He stood up. "I've never done anything like this before, Faust, and I'm not sure why I'm doing it now. Don't make me regret it."

"You won't, sir. I promise."

I couldn't control myself. I sang in the shower at the top of my lungs. The guys must have thought I was crazy. I had hardly spoken to anyone for weeks and there I was crooning away. But I didn't care what anybody thought. First the fight, then Sharkey going down for the year, and finally Raible. Maybe they weren't just coincidences. The whole thing was impossible, but I was so incredibly happy I decided if I had sold my soul, my only regret was that I hadn't done it sooner.

I got dressed and went to the bus stop. The sun was out and big white clouds were racing across the sky. The grass was wet and the sunshine made it sparkle like the Most Valuable Player trophy they give you after you lead your team to a 24–0 season.

After dinner I gave my mother the basketball forms.

"I thought you missed the tryouts."

"I did, but there was an injury and they need a guard, so the coach bent the rules for me."

She took the papers out of the envelope and started flipping through them. "That was lucky," she said, "but then you're due for a little good luck. I'll have Dr. Browner fill out the medical form and I'll talk to your father about the insurance. When do you need these back?"

"I'd like them by Monday," I said. "I can't practice until they're returned."

"Monday? That's a little quick." Then she gave me a little wink. "I'll see what I can do, though."

4

I had a pit in my stomach before that first practice. I didn't know Raible's routine; I didn't know the plays; I didn't even know the names of all the guys on the team. I actually broke into a cold sweat sitting on the bleachers waiting for the whistle to blow. I hadn't come up with any sensible explanation for what had happened in the Ballard gym, but there definitely wasn't any devil giving me power that day, or the next few days either, because I stunk up the gym.

Raible's plays were fairly standard, but there were more of them than we ran at Emerson. Besides, every coach has a few wrinkles of his own. I kept messing up on the back screens he wanted me to set. And sometimes as I was bringing the ball up court during a scrimmage, he'd yell a number and I'd totally blank out on what the play was. At the beginning of the week he'd stop and have the team walk through it again for me, but on Wednesday he sat me down and made me watch a third-string forward play my position. "Pay attention," Raible shouted when he caught me looking at the clock.

He came over to me afterward. "I thought you said you played on a team in Boston."

"I did. I was the two guard. I led the team in scoring."

"That must have been some team," he said sarcastically.

On the bus ride home John tried to cheer me up. "It's your first year here. Besides, you missed two weeks of practice. It'll come."

I shrugged. "I don't know. If it doesn't come quick, Raible's going to send me to the junior varsity. I can feel it."

John opened up his notebook and started putting

down little X's and O's. "Let's go over the plays now," he said.

I probably wouldn't have survived if it weren't for those sessions with John. He quizzed me every morning and afternoon on the bus. Little by little, I got the plays down. And it showed. Sometimes it took a second before I remembered what play I was supposed to run, and that slowed everything down, but at least Raible wasn't yanking me off the court.

On the day before Thanksgiving, school let out at noon. Raible held a short practice. That scrimmage was the first time I didn't have to think at all; I just played. And with me completely in the flow, the guys on the second unit really went after the starters. We lost, but only because Raible would never give us a call. We outhustled and outplayed them, but he made sure they won anyway. Around one o'clock he yelled, "Shoot ten free throws and shower up." Then he beat it out of the gym.

The other guys took off, too. But I hung around, mostly to work on my jump shot. I'd been working so hard to fit in with the team, I hadn't had time to think about my own offense.

I didn't work my way around the key or do anything systematic like that. That's not how shots come in a game, and I was working on game situations. After about half an hour, I decided to practice some three-pointers. I moved out past the top of the key and swished one from there. The spin was perfect and the ball came right back to me as if it were on a string. I was all set to fire up another one when I stopped dead in my tracks. I was standing at exactly the same spot on the court and the ball had come back in exactly the same way as it had that day in Ballard.

That afternoon in the empty gym was never totally out of my mind. You don't stop thinking about things like that. I knew it all had to be a fluke, that the devil couldn't really be helping me out. But it was weird how quickly everything had turned around. I wasn't on the verge of being cut anymore. If I kept outplaying Stamets, Raible would have to move me up to the first string. It was hard not to wonder a little. So when I found myself near that spot I moved away. It was no big deal. Lots of players are superstitious about small things.

It seemed like one day I was alone in my room contemplating a year without basketball and the next I was in uniform at a pep rally on the day of the first game. I vaguely recall stuffing myself on smoked ham at Thanksgiving dinner, but that's about the only nonbasketball event I remember from those weeks. I don't know where the time went, but it went.

At the rally, the cheerleaders came out and kicked their legs while the rowdy guys sitting on the top row of the bleachers whistled and the rah-rah types on the bottom row clapped their hands. After the cheers Coach Raible gave a speech. It was full of clichés about playing to develop character but playing to win, too; about the honor of representing the school; and about the importance of student support. Then they introduced us one by one and the band played the fight song. I was glad when all the hoopla had ended so I could hustle out to the bus and go home.

My father had promised to come to the game, but when it came time to get in the car he had an excuse — as usual. "I'd love to go out, Joe. But I have to write a speech for the Lasker Award ceremony. If I don't do it now, it won't get done. I'll see the next game."

There was always something.

In the car my mother wanted to know how I was feeling. I tried giving her the "Everything's great!" routine, but she wasn't buying it.

"Your father really does have to work. All week he's talked about your game. He wanted to see it very badly. I hope you're not angry or hurt."

"I'm not. Besides, he's not going to miss much. I'll be lucky to play five minutes."

"I'm sure he'll see your next game."

"It's no big deal either way, OK?"

After that, we listened to the radio and talked about the traffic. Since it was a Wednesday night, commuters were still jamming the bridge. We didn't reach Eastside until ten after seven. I was the last guy in the locker room, and Raible looked at his watch and then scowled at me. I could tell he was feeling it. He paced back and forth like a caged orangutan, half-moons of sweat under his arms. At seven-twenty he called us to the chalkboard and started diagraming all the plays. I guess he thought he was clearing things up, but he was just confusing us, making us nervous. Only John seemed calm, and I don't think he was listening. You can't learn anything from a bunch of talk before a game, but coaches can't help blabbing away.

At seven-thirty Raible stopped and we went into the wrestling room and stretched. I liked stretching on those cool mats, feeling my muscles loosen up little by little.

Fifteen minutes later we walked out of the quiet wrestling room and into a packed, noisy gym. The cheerleaders made a path for us and as we ran onto the court the place exploded. The band took up the fight song and the clapping became rhythmic. I felt as if my heart were pumping pure adrenaline. As we split into two lines, an insane urge to try to slam-dunk the first lay-in came over me, but I fought it back. I hadn't tried dunking since that day in the summer and I could see myself ending up flat on my back.

We went through the line five times before we switched to a little passing drill. I don't like passing drills before games. The winner is the team that scores the most points, so I like to spend those last minutes shooting. But every coach I've ever had has wanted to show the fans that he stresses teamwork.

So we passed it around when we should have been nailing fifteen-foot jumpers.

It was seven fifty-five before we began to shoot around. I was long with everything. Too much adrenaline can be just as bad as being flat for a game. Everybody else was missing, too.

Next came the horn and the introduction of the starting lineups. As the guys ran out one by one, the drummer beat on his bass drum and the crowd went crazy. You're not supposed to think this way, but I was suddenly glad I wasn't starting. I was too tight, and when I tried to remember the plays I went blank on all of them. Sitting on the bench for a game or two wouldn't be the worst thing in the world. I'd get some playing time, sooner or later.

5

The Ingraham guards were taller and stronger than either Stamets or Doyle. They set some nice little down-screens against our man-to-man that freed them on the baseline for some easy hoops. We were down 10–2 before Raible called time-out.

Like all the guys on the bench I was ready for a little playing time, but all Raible did was switch to a two-three zone defense. It was smart basketball even though it didn't do me any good. Our forwards, Ray Snellinger and Alex Reynolds, worked with John to dominate the boards. The Ingraham guards were having no luck shooting over the top. When the first quarter ended, it was only 14–10, Ingraham. I hadn't played a minute. None of the second string had.

That's what hurt us in the second quarter. The Ingraham coach was shuffling in fresh legs all the time. Two minutes into the period, their guard popped an outside jumper over Stamets and then stole a lazy pass and went coast-to-coast for a lay-in. I looked down the bench at Raible just as he turned to look at me. But instead of giving me the nod he looked quickly back at the court.

When Raible finally took Stamets out, there were only two minutes left in the half. And it wasn't me, but Burns who went in. Ingraham had all their starters back and, well rested, they dominated the game.

Snellinger and Reynolds could barely get up and down the floor, let alone shoot and rebound. Doyle was exhausted and Burns, though fresh, had a bad case of first-game jitters. Even John was laboring. There were twelve of us on the team, but Raible had played a running game and used only six. It was worse than stupid; it was a massacre. 40–22 was the score at the half.

In the locker room Raible raved about reaching down and gutting it out. It was comical. The starters were so blitzed they paid no attention. The rest of us just nodded, not a drop of sweat among us.

Raible went to the blackboard, diagramed the two-three defense, and explained how they were beating it. "Don't move your arms," he shouted, "move your feet!" I looked around at the starters. They all knew how to play the two-three. They were just too tired to play it well.

That's when John spoke up. "Coach," he said, "if they keep running fresh guys at me, I'm going to need a blow. All things equal, I can burn both of those guys. But when they're rested and I'm dead, they can take me."

Raible glared. "Are you trying to tell me how to coach?"

There was an uneasy silence.

"I'm saying that they're wearing us down."

"Do me a favor, Lustik. Don't say anything. Just play. I'll do the coaching, understand?"

When we filed back onto the court we were a different team than the one that had run out with so much hope just an hour earlier. No cheerleaders jumped to see us. No rhythmic clapping cascaded down from the bleachers. It was halftime of the first game and our heads were hanging low. The fans had given up on us, our starting center was in the coach's doghouse, and we were losing by twenty to a mediocre team. It promised to be a long season.

6

I'd never liked Raible, but when he started Jason Maier at center in the second half, I knew he was a small man. John had told the truth and Raible couldn't bear it. So he benched him. Raible played John when he was exhausted and sat him down when he was rested. Smart coach.

But basketball can be a strange game. For no good reason, we did a little better at the start of the third period. Maier got the tip and Reynolds drove for a bucket off a quick pass. Doyle made a nice steal at half court and took it in. When Ingraham's center missed a hook and Snellinger gobbled up the rebound and found Stamets with a full-court pass, it was 40–28 and the gym exploded.

The Ingraham coach called time to calm his players down. When they came back on the court, they worked a little screen for their shooting guard. He hit a jumper from the free-throw line and our streak was over. The pattern of the first half slowly repeated itself. The Ingraham coach substituted freely. Raible got John back out there, but that was our only substitution. Our guys had heavy legs and they couldn't cut into the lead. With two minutes left in the third quarter of a 52–38 game, Raible finally called my name.

I went in for Doyle at point guard. The other guys were drenched in sweat, but I was cold and tight. I didn't even feel like I was on their team.

The first time down I tried to take the baseline with a quick move. I imagined myself swooping in for a reverse lay-in, but instead I lost control of the ball and fumbled it out of bounds. Then on defense

I reached in and committed a stupid foul. Luckily, the Ingraham player missed the front end of the one-and-one. Snellinger rebounded and hit me with the outlet. I took it right up the gut, spotted Stamets on my left, and fed him a soft bounce pass. Two points.

Ingraham turned it over, and the next time down I broke behind a screen and popped in a little jumper from just inside the free-throw line. I felt the sweat under my arms and on my forehead. The spring was back in my step. I was in the flow, and for the next minute and a half we took it to them. At the end of the third quarter we'd cut it to 57–48.

But when the fourth quarter began, I was back on the bench. Raible also sat down Stamets, Snellinger, and Reynolds. He had John and Doyle out there surrounded by the deep bench. The guys had never worked as a unit in practice, and it showed. In two minutes Ingraham ran off six straight points, and if they hadn't blown two lay-ins it would have been ten. The lead was back up to 63–48 when Raible finally got his best five on the court.

John stayed in at center. Doyle and I were the guards, Snellinger and Reynolds — both slightly rested — were the forwards.

I've got to give Doyle credit. I was the only guy out there who wasn't on the starting unit, but when I flashed across the key, he hit me with a nice pass and I sunk a short hook. 63–50. Ingraham's center tried to baseball the inbounds pass the length of the court. He had a man open, but he threw it too far, and our charge was on.

For the rest of the game everything went right. We all worked together — and hard. John and Snellinger controlled the boards; Doyle controlled the flow; Reynolds scrapped for the loose balls; and I hit the outside shots.

Ingraham didn't completely collapse. They called one time-out, and then another, but the tide had turned. It was 65–57 with four minutes left; 67–62 with two forty-three remaining; 70–67 with a minute to go.

They went into a four-corners stall to milk the clock. We came out of our zone and pressed them. They tried a backdoor play, their center breaking behind John. The guy was wide open and for an instant I thought all our hard work was down the drain, but John somehow managed to get a fingertip on the ball and there was Reynolds to save it from going out of bounds. Doyle took off. Reynolds hit me at center court and I went crosscourt to Doyle with a perfect pass for the puppy: 70–69 with eighteen seconds left.

They tried to run out the clock, but we trapped one of their forwards down in the corner. No foul, just pressure. The ref was counting down five seconds. The Ingraham player panicked, leapt up in the air, and threw a wild pass toward center court. I was lurking at the free-throw line, anticipating just that kind of pass. I broke across the top of the key, intercepted it, and was gone for the easy lay-in. As the ball floated through the net, the clock ticked down to 00:00. 71–70! We had won! Raible was jumping up and down. The cheerleaders were doing cartwheels across the floor. The band played the music from *Rocky*. The place went completely crazy. And I was in heaven.

I was still sky-high when I got in the car twenty minutes later. My mother hugged me. "That was the most exciting game I've ever seen," she said. "Better than college, the pros — it was the best! I was so proud of you. You were the star out there."

I was smiling so much it hurt. But when we hit the freeway, I took a deep breath and suddenly felt exhausted and strangely confused. The road was dark and as we reached the rise before the bridge, my mother's words — *You were the star* — brought me back to that empty gym and those ten perfect shots. I thought about the game; I thought about my game. It had all come together pretty quickly. Usually it takes time to develop teamwork, to learn your teammates' moves, to operate as one. I hadn't spent any time with the first unit, yet we had played like we'd been together for years.

When we got home, my father was drinking coffee in the kitchen, the typed pages of his speech all over the table. Once he heard how we had come from behind and how I was the hero, he wanted details. "Tell me about it. I want to hear it all!"

I must have seemed like a miserable son to him. I grunted my way through a brief description and then went to my room. It's hard to talk about the things you do really well. It wasn't the baskets or the steals that made the game exciting. It was the feeling — the feeling that came over me and the rest of the guys, the feeling that somehow got into the crowd and then came back down to us. It made us more than ourselves, better and purer. My father was too much of a scientist to understand feelings like that, so why try to explain?

Once I was upstairs I opened up *Dr. Faustus*. It sounds corny, but I reread the part where Faustus has his vision of hell. He sees people being tossed about on pitchforks, being broiled over coals, and other stuff like that.

I must have read that passage four times. Sometimes it seemed terrifying. But then I'd read it again and the whole thing would seem ridiculous. Who could really believe in a hell full of fire and brimstone and pitchforks and little devils with pointy beards and long tails?

Then I remembered an old episode of "The Twilight Zone." This playboy dies and goes to heaven. There are parties all the time. He drinks the best wine, always wins at poker, and gorgeous women put the make on him. Everything is perfect, so perfect that he gets bored. "I'd like to visit hell for a while," he says to the angel in charge. "It's too dull here."

"My friend," the angel says, "you are in hell."

7

That next day was a shocker. I was totally unprepared to be the campus hero. Kids who'd never had a good word for me came up and patted me on the back.

"Great game!" . . . "Unreal!" . . . "Awesome!"

Even some of the teachers treated me differently. In history class, after I'd given a basically incoherent answer to a question about Patton, Kerry said, "Excellent, Joe. Right on the mark." And Anyati didn't force me to my knees even though I missed two straight problems.

In fact the whole school, which had always felt so strange and cold before, now glowed with an inner warmth. It was as if it had shrunk down to the size of a cozy living room. A huge fire roared and an amber light fell on everyone, but most particularly on me.

That day in English class we finally reached the climax of the play, the part where Faustus gets dragged down to hell. It didn't make a whole lot of sense to me, so I raised my hand.

"I don't understand why Faustus just doesn't repent at the end. He doesn't have to burn. If he repents, he gets the best of both worlds: he uses the devil's power for twenty-four years and he goes to heaven anyway."

Miss Mitchell nodded. "That's a good point. And it brings up one of the major issues of the play. Why doesn't Faustus repent?" She looked around the room. "Any ideas?"

As usual, Mary Staraska's hand shot up, but Miss Mitchell called on Sheila McMahon, then John, and finally Eddie. None of them had an answer. Frustrated, she finally nodded to Mary.

"The whole time Faustus uses the devil's power," Mary said, "he slowly loses his own. By the end he's completely under the devil's thumb. Faustus doesn't repent because he can't repent."

"Does that make sense to you, Joe?" Miss Mitchell asked.

I shrugged. "Not really. When you're reading the play, it doesn't seem like Faustus changes that much. He's still basically the same person at the end that he was in the beginning. It's not like he's possessed or anything."

"That's the point, though," Ryan Blake chimed in. "The devil is clever. He acts like he's the servant, and the whole time he's the master. The way I look at it, the devil's power works on Faustus almost like heroin works on an addict. He always thinks he can break free, that he doesn't need it, but it's always tomorrow when he plans on going straight."

I didn't say anything, but I wasn't convinced. Heroin addicts are always talking about quitting. It's just that their bodies won't let them. All Faustus has to do is say he's sorry one time and he's off the hook. How much willpower does it take to do that?

8

That day at practice Raible moved me to the first string. I tried to act nonchalant, but my heart was pounding. Everything kept falling my way, but I didn't want to dream up reasons that weren't there. I'd had a good fourth quarter, and Stamets was struggling.

Doyle played the point, and that made things awkward for me. The off guard is supposed to shoot, but taking a lot of shots isn't the best way to get in good with your teammates. Those four guys had played together for years. I didn't want to seem like I was muscling in and trying to take over the team.

So I didn't shoot much during our scrimmages. I was trying to feel my way into the unit. I had to earn their confidence, and that was going to take some time. Lots of guys have one big game; I wanted to be first-string all season.

But the guys on the second unit weren't stupid. Once they recognized that I was passing up my shot, they collapsed into the key. The whole middle was clogged, and none of our big guys could do a thing. Our practices were sluggish.

Our second game was on Thursday. I was more nervous than I'd been for the first one. This time I was starting. This time the pressure was on me.

There was no practice on game days so I got home early. My father was sitting on the sofa reading his mail. I asked him if he was coming to the game. "Is it tonight?" he exclaimed. "I thought it was tomorrow. I agreed to an interview with KCTS at eight o'clock. There's no way I can cancel now. I'm really sorry, Joe."

"That's OK," I said.

"Good luck, though! You'll do great. I know you will."

The atmosphere in the gym that night was entirely different. In the opener, the crowd had been loud, but not nervous. Nobody had expected us to beat a Seattle Metro team. The volume had been fake; the people had cheered just to hear themselves cheer. Now it was quieter. The crowd was hushed because they thought that maybe, just maybe, we were a good team. The fans made less noise, but they cared more.

We were playing Collins Academy, a small school for brainy kids. They'd gone 14–10 the year before, not bad considering their enrollment. Raible told us to expect a tough game.

They controlled the opening tip and worked it around the perimeter for almost a minute before springing one of their forwards low for an easy bucket. I was so tense I forgot everything. I took the inbounds pass, raced the length of the court, and threw up a twenty-foot jumper that bricked off the front of the rim.

Down they came. They ran a motion offense and

took their time. The crowd stomped in displeasure, but once again Collins scored — this time on a short jumper from behind a double screen.

After their second hoop I let Eddie run the plays. Collins was playing a two-one-two zone and they were really packing it in. The outside shot was there, but that whole first quarter I passed it up. Instead of shooting I'd try an entry pass to John, or I'd whip the ball back to Eddie and let him move it to Ray on the weak side or try to penetrate himself.

The Collins players weren't real gifted, but they played smart. They knew if they tried to run with us we'd blow them out of the gym, so they took some time off the clock every time they touched the ball. You can't score if the other team has got the ball, and that whole first quarter it seemed like they had it. We were down 12–7 when it ended.

In the huddle Raible kept yelling that we had to pressure them more, and then he said we had to take our time and get good shots. I couldn't figure what he meant, because if you're up in their faces on defense then you should run every time you get the chance. I looked around at the other guys, and they looked confused, too.

As we walked onto the court for the start of the second quarter, John pulled me aside. "Forget Raible. When your shot is there, take it. It'll open things up for the rest of us."

The first shot I took in that second quarter was way short, almost an air ball. As I backpedaled on defense John told me to relax. "And keep shooting. They'll drop for you."

He was right. I buried six out of nine that quarter. We took the lead at 20–18, and in another minute stretched it to 26–19. Their coach called time, and when they came back out they were in a man-to-man defense. They'd wanted a slow tempo, but my outside shots had forced them out of their zone. They had to run with us, and they didn't have the horses.

In the second half we slapped the press on and they fell completely apart. Reynolds and I would do a double-team trap on the guard with the ball. If one of us was able to strip him, we'd hit Doyle at center court and he'd run the ball right down their throats. I loved filling the lane, taking the soft bounce pass from Eddie, and going up for the easy lay-in. It was like practice, only better, because the crowd was there to cheer.

By the end of the third quarter we were up 52–34, and our lead was 65–40 when Raible turned the game over to the subs midway through the fourth quarter. We came out to a standing ovation.

In the shower we whooped it up. Alex got his towel wet and started snapping it at anybody within range. Pretty soon four or five other guys had done the same thing, and there was a general war going on. I was stung a couple of times, but nothing ever hurts too much after a victory.

I was almost dressed when the team manager

came in with the stat sheet. He handed it to Eddie, and Eddie read off our point totals. When he reached my name, he stopped.

"Holy smokes, Faust, you had thirty points! And listen to this shooting. Twelve of sixteen from the field, including two three-pointers, and four for five from the foul line. This must have been the game of your life, or did you rack up these numbers all the time in Boston?"

I felt everybody's eyes on me. I couldn't believe those numbers myself. Eddie handed me the stat sheet, and they added up just the way he said they did. When I gave the paper back to him I tried to shrug it off. "You keep setting me up for lay-ins and I'll score thirty every time out."

Right then Raible walked in and grabbed the stat sheet out of Eddie's hand. "You guys adding up your points so you can brag to your girlfriends in the back seat of your cars?" he barked. "I suppose next game you'll be counting your points on your arm." Then he paused and looked around at us. "This is a team game and don't forget it."

After that we dressed quietly. But I kept thinking about the numbers Eddie had read off. They were incredible. I had gotten a lot of easy shots, though. And besides, the off guard is supposed to score.

When we got home that night, a strange thing happened. My mother told me there was a treat for me in the refrigerator. I looked in the freezer compartment, expecting to find ice cream.

"Not there," she said as she opened the crisper and took out a plate of the reddest, plumpest grapes I'd ever seen. "I found this wonderful stall at the Pike Place Market that carries fresh fruit from around the world. They had peaches from Chile, jackfruit from Thailand. I got grapes because I know they're your favorite."

She put the plate down on the kitchen table, and I bit into the biggest, ripest grape I could find.

"These are delicious. Where are they from?"

"India."

I felt my face flush. I stood up.

"Aren't you going to have any more?" my mother asked.

I shook my head. "They're great. They really are. But I'm so tired I can't enjoy them. I think I'd better go to bed."

9

"Joe's our scorer. Doyle, make sure you feed him the ball. Lustik, Snellinger, Reynolds: you guys set screens for Joe and then hit the boards. I don't want any of you shooting outside!"

That was our plan for games three and four against Issaquah and Orting. It wasn't much of a strategy, but it worked. I burned the nets like I'd never burned them before. Anything inside the three-point line was automatic; it didn't matter if there was a hand in my face or not. Even when I threw up a bad shot I sometimes got the roll. I scored thirty-two on Wednesday afternoon and thirty-five on Friday night. The Issaquah gym was empty but the Friday game was at Eastside and the crowd roared, "Faust! Faust! Faust!" when I came out in the fourth quarter.

"Are we really this good?" I asked John after the locker room had cleared out on Friday.

He gave me a strange smile. "The question isn't whether *we're* really this good, it's whether *you're* really this good. I'll tell you this, if you keep scoring thirty points a game and making seventy percent of your shots, we're going to keep winning." Then he slapped me on the back, picked up his equipment bag, and went out the double doors.

After he left I sat alone in the locker room and tried to piece together just what had happened in that dirty old gym. Ten shots in a row — big deal. Once I made twenty-nine free throws in a row. But that day in Ballard I'd been standing above the top of the key and the gym had been pretty dark. The ball had just kept coming right back to my hands after every shot. That had never happened before. And then there was that weird mist.

I wanted to laugh the whole thing off. I wanted to believe it was just a coincidence that everything started going right for me the day I made my vow in that empty gym. But if I had sold my soul to the devil, laughing it off was exactly what the devil would want me to do. I'd fall right into his hands.

The day after we beat Kent for our fifth victory, Miss Mitchell passed out copies of *A Christmas Carol* and announced that this was the last day we'd be discussing *Dr. Faustus*. A small cheer went up around the room, and she grimaced. "Don't get too excited. You're still going to have to write a short paper, and there will be questions about it on your final exam."

That afternoon she wanted to discuss what Faustus loses besides his soul. I thought it was an odd question, and so did everybody else. "He doesn't lose anything," one girl said. "He just gets the devil's power."

"Are you sure? Think about his relationship with other people."

There was silence for a long time. Not even Mary Staraska or Ryan Blake had anything to say.

"OK," Miss Mitchell said, "try it this way. Does Faustus have any friends?"

That was easy, so I raised my hand. "Other than the devil, no. But he didn't have any friends before he sold his soul. It's not like he lost them."

"Why doesn't he ask the devil for some kind of human friendship? He can get anything he wants. Wouldn't you think he'd want that?"

Again there was a long, awkward silence. Nobody knew what she was driving at. I heard someone's stomach growl just before Ryan Blake popped his hand into the air. "I get it!" he yelled, startling the kids who had almost nodded off. "Once Faustus sells his soul, he's cut off from other people. He's different from everybody and he knows it. In a way he's not even human. In the beginning he doesn't have friends; once he sells his soul, he can't have friends."

Miss Mitchell smiled, pleased with what he had said, but it didn't sit well with me. If the devil was controlling things, fixing things, then I wasn't really part of the team. The guys didn't know it, but all the pats on the back and the high-fives and low-fives were lies. I wasn't part of anything.

10

My father didn't make it to even one of my games, but he did read the box scores in the paper. "You're really racking up the points," he said at breakfast on Saturday morning. I nodded, and then he started talking about the Lasker Award and the plans for the trip to Boston. They were leaving December 17 and returning the twenty-second.

"If you have any friends you want to visit, write them and tell them you're coming," my father said as he poured sugar on top of his Grape-Nuts. "You must have buddies you're anxious to see."

It was a shock, right out of the blue. It had never occurred to me that I would go to the award ceremony. He was always winning awards, and I'd never gone before. I'd never even been asked. Now, right at the beginning of my senior year of basketball, he expected me to miss my games.

"What about school?" I said. "What about basketball?"

"You'll only miss a few games, and you can bring your books. We'll have a great time."

"I've never been to any of your other meetings," I blurted out.

My father looked away, hurt.

"Joe," my mother said, "I don't think you understand what the Lasker Award is. It is one of the highest awards a scientist can receive. It's like winning the NBA title. Your father has done that. He's won. You don't want to miss that, do you? You may not think you want to go, but when you get older you'll be glad you did."

They both stood up in that way of theirs that means the conversation is over, that everything has been settled.

"Thanks a lot," I said. "Why don't you just come right out and say that nothing *I* do is important?" I stared right at my father. "You haven't bothered to come to one game all year, but you'll drag me three thousand miles to some little hall and make me stand and clap for you."

I stopped, but for once he didn't say anything, so for once I was able to finish. "Let me tell you something, Father," I said in a shaky voice. "You should watch me play basketball. Basketball is the only thing I do really well. If you saw me play, you'd be proud of me. I know I'm not what you had in mind, but I'm the only son you've got."

With that I left the kitchen. I was so angry my whole body was shaking. I went up to my room and fought down the choking feeling in my throat.

I thought I would just stay in all day and think. But I got bored sitting up there, so around noon I slipped down the stairs. I figured I'd go over to Loyal High and blow off steam by shooting some baskets. I didn't make a sound, but my mother must have been watching for me. She stopped me on the porch and told me she'd canceled my reservation. "You can still change your mind. Talk to your teachers, talk to the coach. See what they say."

I nodded, but I wasn't going to talk to anybody.

"I'm going to go shoot some hoops, now. I'll be back later."

I should have been ecstatic. I'd won a victory at home over my father — and that was a rarity. But I didn't feel much like celebrating.

I hadn't lied. Everything I'd said to my father was true. But I still felt awful, maybe because he could have said the exact same things to me. I never paid attention to what he did. That was partly because it was so hard to understand what he was doing. But occasionally there'd be articles in the newspaper that I could have read. My mother always cut them out for me. I'd stuff them in my pocket, and sometimes I'd even read the first paragraph. But most of the time I'd forget about them and then trash them when I emptied my pockets.

I was practicing free throws when I heard the ball bounce. I turned around and saw Ross. I didn't know what to do or how to act, whether to ignore him or take a punch at him. He gave me a vague nod and dribbled by me for a lay-in. He could have at least gone to another hoop to shoot, but he didn't. It was certain *I* wasn't moving.

"I never expected to see you here," he said as he retrieved his ball.

"Why not? It's a free country."

Ross shrugged his shoulders. We shot in silence for a few minutes. He was making everything; I couldn't hit a thing.

"Why did you do it?" I finally asked.

"Do what?"

"Don't play dumb with me. You know what I'm talking about."

Ross stopped shooting. "You make me laugh. You act like I killed somebody — a few bushes, a couple of burning sticks. I'll admit the rock through the window was too much, but that wasn't my idea. Where was the harm?"

"Where was the harm!" I yelled. "The harm was in what it did to my parents. You made them so nervous they jumped every time they heard a sound — they still do. That's where the harm is."

Ross swished a jumper and ran down the ball.

"Come off it, Joe. I read that article. I saw the way
you looked at your old man when I ate lunch at
your place. I did you a favor. You hate your old
man's guts."

"That's not true."

"Oh, isn't it?"

"No, it isn't!"

"Fine, have it your way. I don't care."

I was seething inside. If his ball came in my direction I let it go and made him chase it down. He
did the same thing to me. At twelve-thirty Ross
netted a final shot and disappeared into the Loyal
High gym.

I practiced for another thirty minutes. Once I
calmed down I started to wonder if Ross could be
right. Did I really hate my father? Maybe that was
why I felt a little off whenever I saw his name in
the paper, why I couldn't stand the idea of going
back to Boston with him. A lot of things had gone
wrong between us, and I hadn't knocked myself out
trying to make them go right.

11

We played our sixth game Sunday afternoon against
Monroe. It was at their gym. That meant at least
one hour in the car. I told my mother that I could
catch a ride with John, but she insisted on seeing
the game.

"I feel like I'm bringing you luck," she said.

At eleven I found my father at the kitchen table mapping out the roads leading to Monroe.

"You don't have to do that," I told him. "Raible gave us directions."

My father held out his hand. "Great, let me have them."

I was perplexed. "What do you need them for?"

"I don't want to end up on any snowy side roads if I can help it. It is December, you know."

I wasn't sure I understood him right. "Are you going to my game?"

He didn't say anything at first. He just folded the map up perfectly in a way I can never do. "I'm going to all of your games from now on, Joe. You were completely right yesterday. In the laboratory I see my mistakes quickly. But it seems that outside the lab I see them more slowly, if ever. We aren't close, you and I, not like a father and son should be. I want to work on changing that."

Then he stood up, wrapped both his arms around me, and hugged me. I wanted to hug him back, but for some reason I couldn't. My hands just dangled at my side, almost as if they were dead. After about five seconds he let go. I escaped to my room, where I stuffed my equipment bag for the game. He'd never talked to me like that before. What he said was true enough. I didn't feel close to him. He was a great scientist, but he wasn't such a hot father. Still, I should have hugged him back. I should have found some way to let him know he wasn't the worst father, either.

My father is a fast driver, and there wasn't any snow on the road, so we made good time. When I entered the locker room, the only other person there was John Stamets. He had Monroe's schedule out and was hunched over, staring at their roster.

"Are these guys any good?" I asked him. "Can they beat us?"

"Not likely. They're six and one, but they don't have any height. Our big boys should have their way inside." He looked up at me.

"Don't look so disappointed, Joe. Do you want us to lose?"

"What's that supposed to mean?"

"I don't know. Nothing, really. But sometimes you don't seem very happy for somebody who's scoring thirty points a game on an undefeated team."

Just then Snellinger came breezing in. He told a long joke I didn't follow, mainly because I was thinking about what Stamets had said.

Maybe he was right. Maybe a part of me was hoping we'd lose. One loss would settle it. I wouldn't have to think about any crazy deal I might have made in that empty gym. The perfect season would be history. I could relax. I could get on with just playing.

*   *   *

Once we took the court, I kept sneaking peeks into the bleachers to try to find my father. I must have looked right at him five times, but I didn't recognize him because of the way he was acting. He had his arm around my mother and every once in a while he kissed her on the neck. It even seemed like he was tickling her. They were both laughing, acting like kids. For the first time I could imagine them as teenagers making out in the back seat of his car. It scared me a little, thinking about them in that way.

And another thing scared me: he was watching me play. All this time I wanted him to see my games, but when he was there — actually there — it made me incredibly nervous. That's why I got off slowly. I missed my first three shots and started to think that I'd never be able to do anything with him watching. Then I banked in a jumper from twelve feet and settled into the game.

After those first misses, I hit six in a row and nine of ten before halftime. The only one I missed was a fancy-Dan shot I probably shouldn't have tried: John was open for a short jumper, but I threw up a spinning reverse lay-in instead of giving the ball up.

In the third quarter I drilled a three-pointer in the first minute. It gave me twenty-one points and stretched our lead to 41–25. I'd scored thirty or more in every game I'd started, and with my father watching I wanted thirty this time, too. I figured Raible would yank me early in the fourth quarter, so I started rifling them up. My shot selection wasn't too hot, but I was up to twenty-seven points by the end of the quarter. Monroe's fast break had burned us a couple of times, and they closed the lead to 51–41. Actually I was glad — it meant I'd stay in for at least part of the fourth quarter.

They scored the first bucket to cut our lead to eight. "Defense!" the crowd yelled. It was ridiculous: we were bigger and faster and better. I took a sixteen-footer and swished it. That shut them up.

Their coach called time-out. They ran a play for their forward and he popped in a little jumper over Snellinger. "Defense!" the crowd roared again.

Doyle brought the ball into the front court. Right away I recognized that they'd gone into a box-and-one. I was getting man-to-man coverage all over the court while the rest of their team played zone defense. I'd be double-teamed anytime I moved close to the hoop. It's a hokey setup, easy to beat, like all trick defenses. We'd never worked against it in practice, but I knew what to do. I took my man outside, leaving John and Snellinger and Reynolds lots of room to operate in the middle. I'd play the decoy and they'd score.

But for some reason they didn't want to shoot. They kept trying to feed me the ball, and I'd instantly get double-teamed. I'd move the ball back inside and they'd have a four-on-three, but nobody would take it to the hoop. Even John was tentative. Our lead dwindled away until with twelve seconds left one of their guards nailed his second three-pointer in a row and we were actually down by one. Eddie brought the ball across the time line and then Raible called time-out. That first defeat was staring us in the face.

Before the game had started, I thought losing wouldn't bother me that much. But after running the court for two hours, after having the game in hand, the last thing in the world I wanted was for Monroe to steal it back.

"We need a bucket!" Raible shouted over the roar of the crowd and the din of the band. "Joe, try to shake free in the corner."

"They're doubling me, Coach. I'm not sure I can get open."

"Well, do something!" he yelled.

The horn sounded. Eddie inbounded to Reynolds, who hit me at the top of the key. John set a screen for me on the right side. I drove that way. The guy guarding John yelled, "Switch!" and jumped out on me. But my man stayed with me, too, leaving John alone. He rolled to the hoop and I hit him with a bounce pass. No one rotated over from the weak side to pick him up, and his lay-up kissed off the glass and went through for the winning two points. The Monroe fans groaned, but the fifty or so people rooting for us stood up and cheered their hearts out. My father was one of them.

"That was close!" my mother said when I got in the car. "I thought you guys were going to lose."

"It was closer than it should have been, that's for sure."

"Listen to you two," my father said. "You act like you lost. I thought you were wonderful. You scored thirty-one points. Did you know that? The guy behind me said that thirty points in a prep game is unheard of, and you've done it five straight times. You were terrific!"

When we reached Seattle, he took the university exit. I didn't think anything of it until he actually drove on campus. It was after five-thirty and the place was deserted. He parked in front of the Genetics building and jumped out. "Joe, you drive your mother home. I've got a little work to catch up on. I'll get a taxi later."

My mother tried arguing with him. "It's Sunday. Why don't you just come home and relax?"

My father shook his head. "That game was so exciting I'm all wound up. I might as well put the energy to good use."

He disappeared into the building. As we drove home, my mother told me she was worried. "He's not getting headaches anymore, but it seems to me his color isn't quite right."

"There's nothing wrong with him," I said. "He still plays racquetball four times a week. He couldn't do that if there was anything wrong."

My mother gave me a thin smile. "That's exactly what he told me."

12

That Tuesday morning my parents were up early. I hurried downstairs to say good-bye. My mother kissed me on the forehead. "Make sure you watch the interview," she said. "I marked it in the *TV Guide*."

"I won't miss it. I promise."

The taxi driver pulled up and honked. I helped my father carry the luggage out. He wished me good luck and shook my hand. The taxi drove off and my mother waved at me through the back window. It was strangely quiet when I closed the front door.

On Thursday night my mother called to remind me about the interview. "I know," I said, "I wasn't going to miss it."

My father looked good on television. His face was tan and his wrinkles didn't show. I remembered how he'd looked when he left Seattle and I knew it had to be makeup.

There were two other geneticists on the show with him. My father was the one who'd won the award, but the interviewer talked more with the other two men. At first I couldn't figure out why, but as I watched I understood. They smiled and called the interviewer by name. When they explained things, they used regular words like *cancer-causing* and *algae*. My father was more serious. He didn't smile once, and he used words like *oncogene* and *prokaryotes*.

I didn't really follow what he was talking about. I never could follow my father once he got going. But I was overwhelmed, anyway — overwhelmed by all the things he knew, all the facts and formulas and ideas that swirled around inside his brain.

My parents returned Sunday night. We'd won two games while they were gone: 64–44 over Cle Elum and 72–57 over Woodway. They were just ordinary victories over mediocre teams. Nothing strange happened, and I had become determined not to let myself believe the devil was making us win. It was a long season. We could still lose. Being 8–0 didn't mean you were on your way to 24–0.

My parents usually take a taxi from the airport, but I drove out to SeaTac to surprise them. I guess I was a little lonely. My mother beamed with pleasure when she saw me, and I think she even fought down some tears. My father looked glad to see me, too.

"How's your team doing?" he asked.

"Still haven't lost."

"Did you get your thirty points?"

"No, that streak's over."

He nodded. "Well, the important thing is that you won."

I hadn't planned on it, but when we hit the freeway I told him about a big discussion we'd had in Elmer's class. "One kid said that genetics was the coming field, that it would dominate the twenty-first century the way physics has dominated the twentieth."

"That must have raised Dr. Elmer's blood pressure."

"It sure did. He took it as a personal insult. He said that physics is the only science that describes reality."

"What happened then?" my father asked.

I shrugged. "I'd just watched you on TV, so I stole one of your lines. I said that genetics will change the way we think about reality."

My father smiled. "I'm flattered."

When we got home it was only nine o'clock but it was midnight for them. They went straight to sleep. The house was silent, but it wasn't empty. I went to bed around eleven and slept better than I had in quite a while.

13

Christmas is a big deal for most families, but it isn't at my house. It hasn't been since I was ten and my grandfather died. He was my mother's father, and he died right on December 25. Since that year, it's never been the same.

We exchanged gifts in the morning and then went to Lombardi's for breakfast. That afternoon I shot some hoops while my father worked at the university. My mother stayed home and cooked a big chicken for dinner. And that was it.

The next night we went to see *A Christmas Carol* at ACT. Before my mother had left for Boston, she'd seen me carrying the book around. I told her that we were reading it in English, and she asked if I wanted to see the play. "You have to promise me you'll still read Dickens, though," she said. "It's a classic."

"Right. Of course."

But the day the tickets arrived was the last day I opened that book. I had basketball practice every afternoon and I had all my other classes, too. If my grades slipped my father would be on me. I needed to find some shortcuts.

The play wasn't bad and I even got a little choked up when Scrooge becomes a good guy at the end and hugs Tiny Tim and gives Bob Cratchit a raise. It was corny, but it was all right.

Late that night it rained heavily. I lay on my bed and heard it drum against the roof, watched it splatter against the windows. The rain came in waves. It danced under the streetlights and raced down the gutters. The drumming on the roof grew louder and then went quiet before starting up again.

I couldn't sleep, and I found myself wondering why Faustus didn't change at the end and save himself like Scrooge did. Just a few words and he could have gotten off scot-free. For the longest time I couldn't figure it out, but then it came to me. What does Scrooge lose when he repents? Nothing. A few bucks a week to Bob Cratchit wasn't going to hurt him any. Faustus had it a lot worse. If he'd repented, he would have lost the devil's power. All the pleasures, all the control the devil had given him would disappear and he would have to go back to being the unhappy person he was before he sold his soul.

14

That week we easily swept a Christmas tournament in Carnation. We won three games in four nights, all of them played in a tiny little sweatbox thirty miles from Seattle. My father grumbled about the snowy roads, and I hated sitting in a car for two hours every day. I asked John why we were entered in a tournament so far away when there were so many right in Seattle.

"Raible always pads our record," he said. "He'd drive a hundred miles for an easy win."

There was another reason I didn't like that gym in Carnation: it looked and smelled and felt too much like the Ballard gym. Before the opening game there was an eerie mist in the trees, and the next night there was a weird shadow on the locker-room wall. And after we won the title, when I was dead certain I was the last guy out, I heard the thud of a basketball behind me. I turned around, and even called out, but no one answered.

On the Wednesday we went back to school there was a long article in the *Seattle P-I* about Ross and the undefeated Loyal High team. They were ranked first in the state. Eastside was mentioned at the tail end, when they listed the other teams that had a chance for the state tournament. I hadn't even known there was a tournament.

"Sure," John said when I asked him about it after practice, "though they keep changing the format all the time. This year the top eight teams play off in the Coliseum. Don't get your hopes up, though. The big public schools from Seattle, Tacoma, and Spokane dominate. Our league is dog meat. We won't get invited."

"But we beat Ingraham. That's a Metro school. Doesn't that count for anything?"

John shook his head. "Ingraham's never any good. And we beat them by one point in our gym. Not too impressive, if you think about it."

"What if we go undefeated?"

"Then we might slip in," John said. "But let's face it, there's no chance of that happening."

"What do you mean?"

"Be realistic, Joe. Our schedule has been Mickey

Mouse all the way, and look what's happened. Monroe's a crummy team, but when they clamped on that box-and-one we fell apart. Our last pre-season game is with Garfield. They won the state title last year. They lost a lot of guys, but the ones they've got can still play. They'll blow us right out of the gym."

15

Having to play Garfield was bad enough; facing them on their court made it even worse. Garfield was a tough, inner-city school. I didn't have to ask anybody; I knew it was going to be a black team.

Black guys have a psychological edge over white guys. Almost all the great pros are black, and every one of the great leapers is black. Most white people — even liberals like my parents — think of blacks and crime as going together. They don't like to admit it, but they do. So when a white team plays a black team it's doubly psyched out: the white team thinks the other guys are both better and meaner. I know that's how I always felt in Boston, and from the way the guys talked nothing was different in Seattle.

I was totally confused that whole week. Part of me wanted to lose the Garfield game and finally put that November day behind me. It would set the record straight, and it would have been an easy loss to swallow. The way the guys practiced, the way Raible talked, it was clear they all expected to lose. In the shower the day before the game Doyle said he'd be happy if we could keep the score close, and nobody jumped on him. Not one guy thought we had a real chance.

Before the game our locker room was dead. We were corpses. We sat silently and listened to the Garfield players through the thin wall. They were whooping and hollering, ragging one another, getting ready to play. They worked themselves up into such a fever that it became contagious — they pumped that fever right into me. I felt my adrenaline start to flow. I looked around at the downcast faces of my teammates and it suddenly burned me that we were going to roll over without putting up a fight. I had to do something. So when Raible said, "All right, men, let's go!" like he was marching us to our execution, I jumped up.

"Coach," I shouted, "could we have a minute alone?"

Raible was startled and so were the rest of the guys. They stopped in their tracks and stared at me.

"Just to pump ourselves up, like the pros do."

Raible shrugged and then went out the door and left us. The guys all stared at me. I cleared my throat and tried to think of something intelligent to say.

"Everybody thinks these guys are going to kick

our butts. And maybe they will. But let's make sure *they* do it — on the court. Let's not do it to ourselves before we even get out there."

It wasn't exactly the Gettysburg Address, and I felt like a jerk standing there with all the guys staring at me. But then Alex Reynolds yelled, "The boards are mine!" That got the rest of the guys going, and when we took the court we were all hollering about how Garfield had to watch out for us. Our layer of confidence was about a millionth of an inch thick, but it beat going out stark naked.

Garfield came out pressing. They were going for the knockout early, and I knew I had to handle the pressure because if we fell behind we'd never come back. The first time down, I passed over the press to John. He made a great catch on the baseline and hit a little jumper to give us a 2–0 lead.

Garfield took it right to us. Their guards were real quick and Doyle's man blew by him for a matching basket. They slapped the press back on.

Doyle's man was so quick that I had to break the press. Eddie would inbound the ball to me and I'd work my dribble almost to mid-court and then hit Alex or Ray with a hard pass as they cut toward the middle. They'd either feed it back or get across the line themselves.

Garfield wasn't stealing the ball from us, but their press did take me out of the offense entirely. And they ran the fast break so well that both Doyle and

I had to stay off the offensive boards. I didn't take one shot in the first quarter.

But John shot . . . how he shot! He got that first jumper off my long pass, but his other five baskets came on tough shots with one or two guys up in his face. He must have missed half a dozen, too. Still, when you hit fifty percent with two guys hanging on your arms, you're doing all right. We were up 17–12 at the quarter.

Raible rested all the starters for the first two minutes of the second period. It was a stupid thing to do, but Raible never did know how to handle substitutions. The Garfield coach was resting one guard and one forward. His other three starters had already had a blow and they were primed and ready. They zipped off eight straight points before Raible put us all back in again.

John tried to go right back to work, but they were ready for him. Every time he flashed across the key they swarmed. Once I saw what was happening I looked for Ray Snellinger. The double-team on John made it easy for him to post up, one-on-one. I'd feed him the ball down low. He scored a couple of times after his man went for some good head fakes, and when he blew by him for a spinning lay-in the score was tied at 30–30 with forty-three seconds until halftime.

I decided to take a chance. I'd been hustling back on defense for the whole game, and without any pressure the Garfield guards were getting sloppy with the inbounds pass. So after Snellinger's bucket, I snuck back around and picked off a lazy bounce pass. I went right up for the lay-in and felt the contact just as I got the shot off. I was flat on my back when the ball trickled through the hoop. I made the free throw and we were up by three. That's how it stood at the half.

I'd never liked Raible, but I positively hated him during that halftime. He sat us down, gave us a wicked little smile, and told us the game was ours. "Black people don't come back once you get them down. History proves it. I'm not being a racist and I'm not saying that blacks don't have good qualities. I'm just saying that they'll give up now that they're behind."

That was it. That was his idea of coaching. No halftime adjustments, no new strategy — just a little Ku Klux Klan pep talk. Before the game Raible didn't think we had a chance. Now, with a three-point lead, he acted as if we couldn't lose.

I looked around at the other guys. They all knew Raible was out of his mind. We'd run up and down the court with the Garfield players. We'd pushed and shoved them and been pushed and shoved by them. We'd felt their sweat on our skin, and they'd felt ours. We knew they weren't going to quit.

As we headed out for the third quarter, I could tell John was absolutely exhausted and Snellinger and Reynolds weren't in much better shape. All three of them looked as if they'd played a full game, not just one half.

Eddie Doyle noticed it, too. "You and I have got to score some points," he whispered as, we shot around. "Those guys up front are corpses."

"You get the points, Eddie. I'll try to handle the press and stay back on defense."

If you look at my stats for that third quarter you'll think I did nothing. I had no points and no rebounds. But I also had no turnovers and I was bringing the ball up against the toughest press I'd ever faced. Garfield scored only two baskets off the fast break. I broke up two others and drew one charging foul. I wish I could say I made a couple of steals, but those guys weren't going to lose the ball to me. We led 46–42 after three quarters.

As the fourth quarter began, the Garfield fans rose to their feet. They screamed and pounded on the metal bleachers. "Gar-field! Gar-field! Gar-field!" It was a nonleague game, but it now meant every-thing to everybody. The fourth quarter would be a war.

We scored first — Alex from the baseline. Gar-field threw it away on their trip down. Doyle hit John low, but his jumper was blocked. Garfield picked up the loose ball and I raced back expecting the fast break. But they broke their pattern: the guards walked the ball up. We had stopped their running game.

Their set offense was good, but it wasn't explosive. We were worn to a frazzle and the slower pace let us rest a little. And as the game slowed down, the crowd quieted.

The momentum went back and forth, but we always held the lead. Then, with three minutes left, they had two breakdowns in a row. Reynolds stole a bad pass and drove the length of the court for an uncontested basket. On Garfield's next trip, their center tangled up with John underneath. John did a little play-acting and the ref bit and called the foul. Garfield's coach came running onto the court and got hit with a technical. I swished the free throw and Eddie buried an outside jumper right after that. We had a nine-point lead with just over two minutes left.

I thought we had it. We all did. Their coach called a time-out and we spent that minute celebrating. I don't know how we could have been so stupid. The Garfield players broke their huddle and came out with fire in their eyes. The crowd went crazy. The press was back on, tighter than ever. We were tired and our concentration had been broken by our early victory party. They scored a quick basket. We tried to slow it down and work the clock. They fouled me but I missed the front end of the one-and-one. Garfield rebounded and ran a perfect fast break. 69–64 with a minute twenty-one left.

Still, we tried to stall. We had worked about twenty seconds off the clock when Snellinger just dribbled the ball off his knee and into the hands of

a Garfield player. They were off again. I backpedaled and tried to anticipate the dish-off. I could see
myself making a great steal. But instead of passing,
the Garfield player just turned on the juice and blew
right past me. 69–66.

I can't even remember all that went wrong in the
next fifty-five seconds, how the score became 69–
68 and how they took the ball back. All I remember
is that with four seconds left I was defending against
a two-on-one fast break that was coming right at
me. I was so tired I could hardly get my feet to
move. They should have scored, but the guy leading
the break dished off a split second too soon. I slid
over to block the lane. "Get your feet set!" my mind
screamed, but I didn't know if I could get there in
time. I saw the Garfield player go up. "Hold still!"
I thought as his knee crashed into my chest just
before he released his shot. We went down in a
heap together. I looked up and saw the ball go
through the hoop and heard the crowd roar.

The ref was blowing his whistle furiously and
pointing at one of us. For one horrible second I
thought he was calling a blocking foul on me. Then
our eyes met and he crossed his arms in front of his
chest and threw them out to his side in that glorious
gesture that means "no basket." He'd called a charge
against the defending state champions at home. It
was the gutsiest call I've ever seen a ref make.

We had beaten Garfield.

We were 12–0.

*   *   *

That night I was exhausted, but I couldn't fall asleep. I kept going over everything that had happened since the beginning of the season. I thought about Sharkey's injury, and the way Raible had broken his own rules to get me on the team. I thought about all the baskets I'd scored on strange rolls, and how I always seemed to know where to be on the court. I thought about the charging call against Garfield and the incredible upset we'd pulled off. Life is full of fluky events that don't mean anything, but how could they all be flukes when they kept happening, when everything kept going my way?

Every player has a bad game, or at least a bad half. Sometimes even Magic Johnson can't hit anything. Yet I was racking up the points and making the big plays game after game. There was just no way I could be so good, so consistent. Not by myself, anyway.

PART
FOUR

1

That next week was finals. There was no school Monday, and then exams were every morning the rest of the week. No games were scheduled and school rules prohibited even practice. So just when we were really pulling together as a team, everything stopped.

I thought my father was going to fall apart that week. He wanted me to study my class work. "High Honors might put you in Stanford," he told me on Monday. But he'd also brought back from Boston this thick paperback that was supposed to help me prepare for the SAT. Whenever he saw me with my textbooks, he worried about the SAT. And whenever I had that SAT book out, he stewed about my finals. I think he would have liked to take a meat cleaver and cut me right in half.

I breezed through the finals in the early part of

the week. It seemed that whatever I studied came up on the tests; and what I skipped, the teachers skipped too.

I thought it was just dumb luck until the history exam on Thursday. But in the cafeteria that morning I found myself studying a passage in the appendix on the armistice of Panmunjom.

"What are you reading that for?" one of the kids in my class asked as he peered over my shoulder. "We hardly talked about it."

"I don't know. Just a hunch."

"There's no way that stuff's going to be on the test. You're wasting your time."

But four of the multiple-choice questions were on the armistice, and in the hall afterward the same guy shook his head when he saw me.

"Are you psychic or something? You must be the only guy in the world who reads the appendix."

My last test was English, on Friday. It covered *Dr. Faustus, A Christmas Carol,* and all the poems and stories from the first half of our literature anthology. If I did well, for the first time in my life I had a real shot at straight A's. That night I reviewed *Dr. Faustus* and reread two short stories and about ten poems. I couldn't reread everything, though, so I was in a sweat that Miss Mitchell would ask about something I'd totally forgotten.

In the morning I felt a little sick to my stomach as she told us we had two hours, wished us luck, and passed out the exam. I looked at the questions, and then looked again. It wasn't just one thing, like on the history exam. I'd reread every single short story and poem she asked about. For the long essay we had to write why Scrooge was saved and Faustus wasn't. That question hadn't really left my mind since that night at the theater. I filled up two pages in no time. The test was easy — too easy.

2

I was home that day before two, and I spent the afternoon in my room listening to records and looking out the window.

I should have been happy. My grades were better than ever, my father was starting to treat me like a person, and I was the leading scorer on an undefeated basketball team that had an outside shot at the state title. But all I wanted was for the year to be over and done with.

The sun came out Saturday. The wind was warm and there were big white puffs of clouds in the sky. I laced up my basketball shoes, pumped a little air into my basketball, and headed over to Loyal High to shoot around.

I'd been shooting for ten minutes when I heard someone dribbling behind me. I knew who it was before I even looked — I could tell from the rhythm of the basketball.

"Hey, how's it going?" Ross said.

"Not bad," I answered coolly. "And you?"

"Can't complain."

We both took a few shots in silence. Then Ross swooped in for a lay-up. When the ball went through the hoop, he caught it, held it, and looked at me.

"Want to go one-on-one?"

"Sure."

We played to eleven. I wanted to stuff him. I wanted to take it to him hard and make him eat dirt. But it didn't work out that way. He was too strong for me inside, and he was quick as a cat. He beat me five straight times. I'd forgotten just how good he was.

When I first saw Ross that afternoon, I thought we might have a serious conversation, that we'd go over everything until we got it straight. But once we started playing basketball, once we both broke a sweat and chased down a few rebounds, once that happened I sensed there was no point in saying anything. We could never be friends again. But on the court we had the basketball and the hoop in common. It doesn't sound like much unless you've played. Then you know.

After the fifth game it started to drizzle. We kept on for a few more minutes, hoping it would stop, but it was winter and the drizzle turned to freezing rain. We had to quit.

We walked down 24th together for a few blocks. At 80th we parted ways. "Tell me something," Ross said as I turned for home. "Does your mother really have naked guys in her room?"

I smiled. "Yeah, she really does."

3

When practice resumed the next Monday, Raible called us together and told us that I was taking over at point and that Eddie was going to move to the second guard. "It's just an experiment," he said.

Instantly I looked at Eddie. I thought he'd be furious, but he gave me a little nod, and I knew Raible had already cleared it with him. I looked around at the other guys. None of them said anything, but I could tell from their eyes they were behind me.

It was what I'd always wanted, right from the start. Scoring points gets your name in the paper, but when you're the point guard, the team is your team. It takes on your personality, and if you win, you feel like the whole game is yours.

I knew what it meant for Eddie to give up his position. He'd been playing with Ray and John and Alex for four years; I hadn't even been playing with them for four months. Those guys were going to let me call the shots, so I owed it to them to call them right.

During practice I made sure everybody was

involved in the offense. I tried to give all of them passes they could reach, but only if they went full bore. It wasn't like the summer when I'd played dumb and made my teammates look bad by being too fancy. I worked to match my passes to their talents. Ray could handle the bullet; Alex couldn't. John could gather in bounce passes in traffic; Eddie panicked and fumbled them away. I noticed everything. I noticed and I remembered. I had to learn their games and they had to learn what to expect from me. Most of all I wanted them to believe that if they worked hard I'd get them the ball. You can't tell your teammates that; you have to prove it to them.

The league opener was on Sunday afternoon. In the locker room before the game the other guys were loose. All week they'd been talking about how lucky we were to open against a dog team. The Hebrew Academy was a small school. Technically, they shouldn't have been in our league at all, but they stayed in because their principal kept hoping enrollment would go up. Raible went through his normal chalk talk and warned us to be ready for a tough game. Snellinger and Reynolds snickered, and Raible caught them.

"Hey, hot shots, there's many a good team that's been knocked off. You're going to have to do more than throw the ball on the court to win this game, and don't forget it."

"Sorry, Coach," Reynolds said, and after that he did his best to put on his game face.

The first time I touched the ball, the guy guarding me sagged off. As shooting guard I would have gone right up with the jumper. But I fought down the impulse and moved the ball around instead. There'd be time to shoot later, once we'd established what we could do.

It didn't take long to find weaknesses we could exploit. John could muscle them inside at will. Ray couldn't score on the post-up because they kept collapsing on him, but when he'd kick it back to Eddie, Eddie would have an open fifteen-footer. I ran a clear-out for Alex a couple of times and he scored once and was fouled the other time.

The Hebrew Academy had some tall players, but not one of them was coordinated. I think they were terrified, too. They'd played all their nonleague games in tiny gyms against small schools. Our place was packed, the band was playing the music from *Rocky* and *Star Wars*. Once we started clicking, they crumbled. All our starters came out near the end of the third quarter when the lead had reached thirty. The crowd cheered us, and we cheered one another.

I scored eight points that game, my lowest total of the season, but the stat sheet after the game was a thing of beauty. The other four guys on the starting unit were in double figures. I'd spread the ball around so that John and Alex both took eleven shots; Ray had nine, Eddie eight.

I was feeling pretty good about the game, but as I left the locker room after the game the Hebrew Academy coach stopped me. "You played tremendous basketball, young man," he said in a thick accent. "What inspires you? Can you tell me that?"

My ears went red. "What do you mean?" I asked.

"You play with such confidence, such knowledge. You look invincible, like you have some secret power. Do you have some secret power, young man?" He smiled as he spoke, but I hurried to the car before he could say any more.

4

We beat St. John's that Tuesday, Bush Friday, and Lakeside the following Sunday. The Bush game was a blowout, but the other two were hard fought. Against St. John's Ray scored sixteen points, including six in the fourth quarter. He dominated the key at the end and we won by eight. The Lakeside game was at their gym. They had a huge crowd that pumped them up and we fell behind early. Fortunately, John had a hot hand. I kept feeding him the ball and he kept us close. Then they went cold in the fourth quarter and we took it to them. After that game, Raible told me I'd reached double figures in assists every game I'd started at the point. Then he waved the stat sheet over his head. "I'll read the rest of you guys your rebounds, steals, and turnovers," he shouted, "but not your points."

My grades came in Monday's mail. I was right — straight A's. I wish I could say I felt like I'd really accomplished something, but the joke was I would have felt better if there had been at least one B.

My father was ecstatic, though. "I knew you could do it!" he said after he'd read the card for the twentieth time. "I say we celebrate. It's your choice for dinner."

I picked Zesto's. My father loved the place as much as I did. I think he snuck there when he worked late. My mother hated the burgers because they were so greasy. She was a good sport, though, and didn't say a word when both my father and I ordered bacon double cheeseburgers, mocha shakes, and large fries. She picked up a stack of napkins and handed them to us. "You'll need them all," she said as she crumbled crackers into her clam chowder.

Afterward we went to Häagen-Dazs. I had a double scoop of chocolate almond, my father had chocolate chip, and my mother had a dish of vanilla. It was cold outside and whenever anyone opened the door a burst of icy air would chill us to the bone. We all laughed every time it happened. An outsider looking at us that night might have said we looked like a perfect family, a family nothing terrible could ever happen to.

5

We were sixteen games into the season and had a spotless record, but we were a nervous team in the locker room before the Bellarmine game. We were playing the defending league champions in their gym. And Eddie told me Eastside hadn't won in that snake pit in twelve years.

John had a thick rubber band that he kept twisting and turning and switching from one hand to the other. He talked nonstop about Bellarmine's center and how the guy had eaten him up the year before. Alex was telling John not to worry, but Eddie looked green and Ray actually threw up. Waiting around before a big game is always the hardest part.

In the first quarter, we all played like robots. I telegraphed a couple of passes and the Bellarmine guards picked them off. But I wasn't the only one who started slowly. Nobody could do anything. Bellarmine should have been crushing us, but they weren't. They couldn't buy a basket. It puzzled me until I put myself in their shoes. We were undefeated; they'd lost twice. They were as afraid of us as we were of them.

John noticed the same thing. On the way out to start the second quarter, he told me to feed the ball inside. "These guys are backing off. We can muscle them."

It worked. I didn't do much that quarter except dump it in to John and Ray and Alex down low.

The jitters were long gone, so those guys pounded the boards and let their elbows fly doing it. We also played tough defense. I got in number forty-two's jersey every time he touched the ball. Once he drove right by me, but as he went up for the lay-in I fouled him so hard he barely got the shot off. I guess I rattled him good, because he missed both free throws. It wasn't exactly dirty basketball, but it wasn't what you would call a clean game, either.

We were up 33–29 when we went to the locker room. Raible liked what he was seeing and didn't want to change anything. "Get the ball low," he shouted as he waved his chalk around.

It had worked for a quarter, but I didn't think it would work for a full game. The Bellarmine coach would make adjustments. Besides, John and Ray each had three fouls and Alex had two.

Sure enough, we were barely a minute into the third quarter when John was whistled for number four. Raible had to sit him down. And with John out, the momentum changed. Now Bellarmine started to take it to us. They were throwing the elbows; they were doing the extra pushing.

The foul trouble hurt. Our big guys had to play a little loose on defense. The Bellarmine center, a big Scandinavian kid named Lars Nielsen, started popping in eight-footers. Bellarmine took the lead at 41–40 and had stretched it to 49–43 by the end of the third quarter.

On the first play of the final quarter, Nielsen

snagged an offensive rebound, made a lay-in, and was fouled by Alex. Nielsen hit the free throw and Raible called time-out. We were down by nine. The gym was rocking. Bellarmine was sky-high.

I stared at each of the guys during that huddle and they all looked beaten. The fire was out, and they didn't seem to care. I knew what was going on inside them because it was going on inside me. Being undefeated isn't all fun. With every victory the pressure builds. A loss takes the pressure off. You lose your perfect season, but you can breathe again. The guys were ready to fold.

Raible was no help. He spent that minute talking about taking good shots and not panicking, but he was talking so fast and so loud that it was clear he was panicked.

When we took the court again, I was as shaky as the rest of the guys. My sweat had gone cold during the time-out, and I had the strong desire to be off the court and out of there. The crowd was screaming, the Bellarmine guys had that cocky bounce in their step and that hungry look in their eyes.

The whistle blew. But just before the ref handed me the ball, I tuned out the crowd, the band, the Bellarmine players — everything. All I thought of was that empty gym, of those ten straight shots, of that perfect rhythm, of that complete confidence. And as I thought of it, the feeling came back.

I took the ball up the right side and faked a pass to John down low. I hadn't shot much all game, so my man went for the fake just a bit. In that split second I was up — free and easy — for the jump shot: two points. That's how the streak started.

Next time down I drove the lane and pulled up for a short jumper just inside the free-throw line: Swish! They turned it over on a three-second violation. I hit a long jumper from the corner, then turned a blocked shot by Alex into a driving lay-in and a three-point play. John fouled out trying to block a Nielsen hook. Nielsen hit one of two free throws, but then I buried a three-pointer from the top of the key. After that it was as if all the other players were in slow motion and only I was moving full speed. I was unstoppable. I knew it and the Bellarmine players knew it, too. The crowd grew quieter and quieter. Snellinger set a screen for me and I used it to drive for a reverse lay-in with the left hand.

They called a time-out and set up a box-and-one defense to try to stop me. It didn't work. I hit a jumper from the left side the first time down, then faked the jumper and drove into the lane for a little running eight-footer which rattled down. Every time I shot, the ball was in the hole. I was magic.

When I was on the court, when it was actually happening, I didn't think about where that magic came from. I just loved having it. I felt a power and a strength flow through me that I never wanted to lose. I was aware of everything — the way the guys were breathing, the squeaking of their basketball shoes. Sometimes I thought I could even hear their heartbeats.

We won 77–70. I was ten for ten from the field — including two three-pointers — and three for three from the line in that fourth quarter. Twenty-five points in one quarter was a league record. So were the ten straight field goals.

Afterward it was like coming out of a trance, or maybe like waking up after being hypnotized. I knew what I had done; I remembered it all clearly. But somehow it didn't seem like it was me that had done it. It was as if a force outside me was using my body. Until that game I'd always felt that somehow I'd be able to keep everything under control. After that night, I wasn't sure.

6

The SAT was Saturday morning in Loyal High's cafeteria. My father was more nervous than I was. At breakfast he kept drilling me on math formulas. "Let the boy eat his eggs in peace," my mother finally said. "Can't you see you're just confusing him?"

The top students had taken the SAT in the fall. Most of the kids in the cafeteria that winter morning were probably in the same boat as me: hoping to sneak into some college with a good senior-year GPA and an SAT score a few precious points higher because of two extra months of preparation. You could feel the tension. John and guys like him would be getting their acceptances in March. We wouldn't hear one way or the other until June at the earliest.

I didn't expect to do particularly well, but as soon as I saw the first problem, I felt an incredible rush of confidence. I worked in a frenzy of concentration, and everything I'd ever learned seemed to click together. I didn't check anything — I didn't feel I had to.

I filled in the last little oval and then looked up. I was the first one finished. There was still an hour left, and all around me heads were down and pencils were bobbing. I moved my answer sheet to one side of the desk and my scratch paper to the other.

Right away I felt that something was off, but it took a while before I figured out what. It probably wouldn't have come to me at all if I hadn't written my name and student identification number on a scratch page just for something to do.

I looked at those numbers, and then I looked at the numbers I'd written when I was working out the math problems. On the math problems I'd put that little line through 7's that Europeans use. I hadn't done that since eighth grade, and there was no little line through the two 7's in my student I.D. number. And all the other numbers seemed a little different, too.

I turned to the end of the math section and looked at the last few problems. They seemed impossible.

Then I paged through my scratch papers and found my work. I couldn't believe what I saw. For problem after problem, there were rows and rows of neat little figures leading to one of the four possible answers. The work was there and it was perfect, but it didn't seem like my work. My head started pounding and I was afraid I was going to black out.

I didn't think that hour would ever pass. After they picked up the tests, I was the first one out the door. I almost knocked over one of the examiners, but I had to breathe fresh air.

I headed straight home. I wanted to get up to my room, shut the door, and think. When would something in my life go wrong? I'd had enough success, enough perfection. It wasn't real, none of it.

I was a block away when I spotted the aide car in front of my house. The red light was spinning round and round, but the siren wasn't blaring. I stood stock-still and watched as the front door flew open and my mother backed out, her hands to her mouth. Next came the stretcher with my father on it.

My mother spotted me and called my name. I ran to her and she hugged me on the front lawn. Out of the corner of my eye I saw the stretcher being lifted into the aide car. I was sure my father was dying — or was already dead.

"He's had a heart attack, Joe," my mother whispered as she squeezed my hand. "They're taking him to University Hospital. You drive — I don't think I can."

We waited for two hours before anyone spoke with us. Finally a doctor called us into his office. "There's no immediate danger," the doctor said. "He's doing as well as can be expected, but he's not out of the woods. If you want, you can see him now."

I don't know what I thought my father would look like, but it wasn't what I saw. He had tubes up his nose and more tubes stuck in both arms. His face was pasty white except for big red blotches on his cheeks. His skin was wrinkled. The pajama top wasn't buttoned and I could see the hair on his chest had gone completely gray.

For the first time he looked old to me. Even if he survived this heart attack, he wouldn't live forever. Of course I always knew my father wouldn't live forever. But it's one thing to know it in your brain and another thing to know it in your heart.

My mother kissed him on the forehead, so I did, too. His skin was cold. I felt sick to my stomach and just wanted to get away, to get out of the hospital and back to the house and up into my room. But my mother sat down and so I sat. We must have stayed for twenty minutes. Finally a nurse came in. "He won't wake up for hours. You should go home and rest. That's the best thing you can do right now."

The whole time we were in the hospital, the whole time I sat in the chair staring at my father, I kept thinking that somehow his heart attack had to be tied in with that promise in the old gym — and that somehow I had to find a way to call the whole thing off. But how do you go back on a deal you're not sure you ever made? And I wasn't sure, not completely. I wasn't sure about anything anymore.

I didn't think I'd be able to sleep at all that night, but I did. It was a black, dreamless sleep and in the morning my mother had to wake me up.

We drove to the hospital right after breakfast. My father looked a little better. He was sitting up; his shirt was buttoned. There were tubes in his arms but none up his nose. He whispered to us between sips of water. To his right were all these fancy machines. Red lights blinked on and off and those blue digital numbers kept changing. Around him were the other patients in the intensive care unit. Most of them were hidden behind curtains. Some had visitors. I wondered how many would live, how many would die.

My mother stopped to talk to the doctor again before we left. I stood off to the side and waited. The doctor said that my father was going to stay in intensive care for the time being.

"He's doing about as well as can be expected."

My mother nodded.

The doctor flipped through the medical chart. "Is there anything else we should know about? Any special stress he's been under recently? Something that might still be bothering him?"

For a split second my mother looked over at me. Then she turned back to the doctor. "He was under more pressure than usual a few months ago, Doctor. But those problems have settled down. I don't think they're on his mind quite so much anymore."

7

For those last two weeks in January, I did everything I could to turn myself into a machine. In the daytime I didn't let my mind wander for an instant. I concentrated on every single word the teachers said, and at practice I worked harder than I've ever worked in my life. But once practice ended, I was the first guy in the shower and the first guy out the door. I knew my mother was waiting for me.

Our routine was always the same. We'd drive to the hospital and visit with my father for an hour or so. When he got tired we'd leave and go out for a quick dinner. I'd go upstairs to my room and study until eleven o'clock.

And every night when I flicked off the light, I'd think I'd pulled it off, that I'd put all thoughts of any pact with the devil out of my mind. I'd fall asleep right away. And then every night, sometimes at two A.M., sometimes later, the same fear would wake me up. Was the devil tricking me? Was he

giving me everything I'd always said I'd wanted —
all the victories and all the glory — and taking my
father's life in payment?

8

We won game eighteen while my father was still in
intensive care, and games nineteen, twenty, and
twenty-one the week they moved him to the regular
ward. A different player led the scoring in each of
the games, and our shooting as a team was over
fifty percent. It was a time of pure joy for the other
guys. They were sky-high after every game.

The whole school was in a fever. There were
banners all over the halls celebrating our victories.
With each game the excitement grew. All anyone
talked about was basketball: the last game, the next
game, and, sometimes, the state tournament. We
were ranked ninth in the state, but every week we
moved up a notch or two as other teams dropped
games. For what it was worth, it was all coming
true.

The next Tuesday we beat St. John's 36–26. The
score was low because they went into a four-corners
stall right from the outset, and they used it even in
the fourth quarter when their only hope was to run
with us. It was a bore to play, and it must have
been a bore to watch, because even their fans booed.

They let my father out of the hospital the next

day. At first I thought it meant he was much better, but when I came home that day it seemed all they'd done was move the hospital room to our house. There was a nurse outside his door, and the tray by his bed was covered with little bottles of pills. The whole house had a different smell, part disinfectant, part roses.

"You look good!" I forced myself to say when I entered his room.

He nodded. "Thanks, Joe. I think I'm coming along." His voice was hoarse and he had trouble clearing his throat.

We talked for about ten minutes, first about school, then about the SAT, and finally about basketball.

"I miss seeing your games."

"You'll be watching me again in no time."

His face went serious. "I know you're just saying that, but you're right. I'll be back on my feet soon, real soon, sooner than you think."

I stood up to leave. "Is there anything I can get for you?"

"I'd like a cigarette. But I'm not going to get one, am I?"

9

Before practice the next day Raible called me into his office and introduced me to a bearded man.

"I'm Roger Bonner." He stood up to shake my hand. "I'm assistant basketball coach at Eastern Washington University. I like the way you play and I thought after practice we could talk about your plans for next year."

"Sure." I thought my heart was going to come right out of my chest.

With Coach Bonner sitting at courtside, Raible was entirely different. He yelled more, ran us harder, and badgered us about executing our plays perfectly. He also kept us forty-five minutes longer. Finally he gave his whistle a toot. "Shoot twenty free throws and shower up!"

Coach Bonner came over to me.

"Would you mind running through a few drills?" he asked.

"No problem."

The other guys gave me little encouraging looks as they disappeared into the locker room. They all knew what was up.

Coach Bonner timed me as I ran lines forward and backward, and he measured my vertical and horizontal leap. Then we sat down on the bleachers and he asked about my grades and my long-term goals.

"You've been straight with me, Joe," he said when I'd finished, "so let me level with you. Cheney is barely on the map, and we don't get the top recruits, the super talents. We never will. So we look for other things. You're probably a step slow, but you've got good basketball sense and you like to compete. Sometimes that's worth more than a step. So I'd like you to visit our campus. It will give you a chance to meet Coach Burns and talk with the players. If you like us and if we like you, then we'll talk scholarship." He stood up and handed me a large white envelope. "There are some brochures in here, and an application form. Think about what I've said, talk it over with your parents. I'll be in touch." We shook hands and he walked out of the gym.

When the door swung closed behind him, I sat alone on the bleachers. I was stunned. All my life I'd dreamed of playing college ball, but I'd thought it was just that — a dream. And now, suddenly, it was right in front of me.

I sat there for a long time. Finally the janitor came in and turned off most of the lights. "Closing up!" he shouted.

I stood up. There were only two lights left on in the gym, and as I started to walk across the court to the locker room to get my stuff, I saw the shadow of the backboard against the gray wall. It was just like the shadow in the old gym in Ballard. The excitement drained right out of me. I would have given anything to go back in time, then, back to November 16 and obliterate those ten perfect shots from my life.

10

"How exciting!" my mother said that evening as she chopped onions for the soup. "Though I must admit I don't know anything about Eastern Washington University. I'm not even sure where it is."

I spread the brochures out on the kitchen table. She dumped the onions into the saucepan and sat down. We flipped through the pamphlets together. The school looked nice enough. There was lots of outdoor stuff to do and Spokane was thirty minutes away. But neither of us was too excited.

"You don't seem sure about this, Joe."

"I guess I'm not," I admitted. "I never really thought I'd be good enough to play college ball. I'm not convinced I am."

My mother put the knife down and looked at me. "Joe, you're down now because of your father, and so am I. But you've got to think about next year. Time doesn't stand still. You've got to make plans and move on."

She went back to chopping. I started to go up to my room, but she stopped me.

"Are you going to tell your father? He's got Stanford on the brain, you know."

"I know. And I'll tell him, but not for a while. No sense in getting him all worked up. Besides, I haven't totally made up my mind."

11

I felt sick to my stomach almost all the time then: morning, noon, night . . . before the games and after them. The only time I felt good was during the games — when I was actually on the court. I still loved playing. Once I broke a sweat my mind turned off. I couldn't think, and for two hours it was as if I were floating in a huge, soundproof bubble that blocked out everything: my father's illness, my unreal run of good luck, everything. The bubble grew larger, went faster, and soared higher with each victory. And it wasn't until afterward, when I was alone in the locker room, that I would think about what might happen when the bubble finally burst.

We crushed the Hebrew Academy on March 1. It was our twenty-third straight victory, but we didn't celebrate much. There was too much pressure and we were all too tense. The day before, the top ten teams had been listed in the paper. Loyal High was still undefeated and was ranked first. But we'd jumped up to seventh. Our schedule was Mickey Mouse and everyone knew it. Still, with one more victory we'd be in the state tournament, too. And once you were in, the rankings didn't mean a thing.

The next day after practice I stayed in the shower a long time. I let the warm water run down over my face and body. I wanted to let that water inside my head somehow. I wanted to wash out everything and start fresh.

*   *   *

My locker was next to John's. When I came out of the shower, he was sitting stark naked on the wooden bench, staring at his clothes.

"What an incredible year this has been," he said. "Incredible! Unbelievable! Unreal! There aren't enough words. When Sharkey went down, I thought we were in for a long season. Even those early wins didn't seem like anything. But when we took Garfield, I knew this year was something special. Now I don't think we'll lose. Sometimes I don't think we can lose."

I didn't say anything. I toweled myself off and started to dress. But John didn't even notice. He was so keyed up he just kept on talking.

"It's like we've become one body out there on the court, with you as our brain. Maybe not the brain. Maybe the heart. Yeah, that's right. The heart. You're the one that keeps the whole thing pumping." He looked over at me. "So take care of yourself, good buddy. We're all counting on you."

That night I lay in bed and had long conversations in my head with everybody: my mother, my father, Ross, John, even Miss Mitchell, for some crazy reason. I explained to all of them how it had happened, how I thought that maybe I'd sold my soul in that old gym and how I couldn't make sense of anything that had happened afterward. They asked a few questions, and when I answered they all nodded their heads and told me that I didn't have anything to worry about, that it was all a figment of my imagination, and that none of them held anything against me.

Then I turned off the light. As usual, I fell asleep right away, but that night I had a strange dream. I was at my grandfather's funeral and was sitting in the front pew between my mother and father. The minister was talking, but I was looking at the casket. Then my mother nudged me. When I looked back at the pulpit, the minister was holding up a trophy and waving me forward. I went to the front of the church, only it wasn't a church anymore, and he wasn't a minister. He was Coach Bonner and I was in Eastside's gym. He handed me the trophy and I held it up over my head as everyone cheered. I caught my mother's eye and she clapped harder. Then I looked for my father, but the chair where he'd been sitting was empty.

12

The Bellarmine game started Saturday at three o'clock. I forced myself to stay in bed until eight. Then I got up and ate a bowl of Wheaties. My father was sleeping, but when my mother came downstairs I asked her if she needed anything done. For the next hour I cleaned out all the kitchen cabinets.

I tried to watch TV then, but ESPN had a golf

match and it was too slow. So I went outside and swept the garage. I checked with my mother at ten. My father was awake, so she said it was OK to start up the lawn mower.

"But are you sure you should do that now? Aren't you going to wear yourself out?"

"I'll be fine."

After I finished both lawns, I got out the edger and did everything, even around the trees. Then I laid down some fertilizer. I didn't stop working until just before it was time to leave. By then I was drenched in sweat. I hustled upstairs and packed my equipment bag. In a few hours the twenty-fourth game would be history and the deal — if there was one — would be done. I couldn't wait for it to be over.

I looked into my father's room before my mother and I left. He was sitting in bed with a book open on his lap, and for a couple of minutes he talked nonstop about getting back to work. He didn't even mention my game, a sure sign he was thinking about it and nothing else. I'd always wanted him to be a fan of mine, but now that he was, it scared me to death. Our game was going to be on the radio. The doctor had ordered him not to listen, but he wasn't too good at obeying doctor's orders.

None of the guys said a word before the game. We all knew what was at stake. We were shooting for the first perfect season in the history of the school. With a 24–0 record, we'd have a lock on a place in the state tournament. But at 23—1, our soft schedule would come back to haunt us. We'd drop to number eleven or twelve and would stay home.

In the locker room you could hear the crowd. Our fans were already on their feet, already cheering. Even the band sounded different. The cymbals clashed louder, the saxophones wailed longer, the drums pounded out a wilder beat. Only the two half-moons of sweat under Raible's arms hadn't changed.

As we ran out onto the court, the cheerleaders started doing flips and somersaults. The fans rose to their feet and chanted "Twenty-four and O!" I spotted my mother right behind our bench.

The horn sounded and we huddled around Raible. Everybody was pumped and ready to go. Everybody but me. I felt sluggish, and seeing how high the other guys were made me feel even lower.

Bellarmine came out sharp as a tack. They went right after John. They'd get the ball to Nielsen, their center, and he'd turn and muscle toward the hoop. In the first four minutes he scored six points and John was whistled for two fouls.

I couldn't get in the flow. My passes weren't bad — it's not like I was throwing the ball away. But they weren't crisp. John had to jump for one, and that gave Nielsen time to get out on him. And twice when Eddie was open I led him too far and he ended up taking off-balance shots. We were down 14—10 at the quarter.

In the first minute of the second quarter, John got whistled for his third foul and had to sit down. With him out, Nielsen went to town inside against Maier. When Nielsen hit a soft hook they led 29–22.

Nobody panicked. I brought the ball down and we worked it around until Ray popped free right under the hoop. I hit him with a bullet pass that went right by Nielsen's ear. It was the first good pass I'd made. Ray went up and banked in the soft lay-in, but when he came down, he landed on Nielsen's foot. The ankle twisted and he writhed in agony. He had to be carried off.

With two of our starters out, Bellarmine really tried to take it to us. In fact, they tried too hard. Nielsen forced up a couple of bad shots, and Maier drew a charge on a two-on-one. At the half, we were only down 33–26.

"Are you OK?" Eddie asked me during the break.

"What do you mean?"

"You seem dead out there."

"I'm fine."

As we huddled before the start of the second half, all the lights went off for a moment, and then thunder rumbled overhead. The rain came a few seconds after that, sheets and sheets of rain that bounced like tiny bullets on the metal roof of the gym.

Raible put John back in and the first time Bellarmine came into the forecourt he picked up his fourth foul. He sat down again. Raible called time-out and the rain came even harder, so hard that we could hardly hear his instructions. The lights blinked and then went out for at least five seconds as more thunder rumbled overhead.

"We're going to a one-two-two," Raible was yelling, "with Joe up top."

More thunder, more lightning, more sheets of rain. With Bellarmine up 44–37, Doyle crashed the offensive boards and caught an elbow. As he lay on the ground, he spit out a mouthful of blood. The ref called time and a doctor came on the court. He insisted that Doyle leave the game. "His front teeth are loose," the doctor shouted at Raible. "He needs to see a dentist right now."

We needed points from somebody, and it was Jason Maier who wanted the ball. "Get it to me," he said as we backpedaled down court. "I can score."

And he did. He missed his first shot, then hit his next three. Because of that little flurry, we pulled to within three with a minute left in the third.

Then disaster struck. Alex Reynolds picked up his fourth foul on a picky little over-the-back call. Compared to the bumping that had been going on all night it was nothing, and Alex slammed the ball down when he heard his number called. That got him his first technical, and when he wouldn't stop arguing the ref hit him with a second one — and the automatic ejection that goes with it. Bellarmine sank two free throws and we were down 44–39 at the end of three quarters.

Raible started John in the fourth quarter. Bellarmine knew he had four fouls, and they brought the ball right to him. Nielsen gave John a little head fake, but John didn't bite. He stood stock-still and Nielsen jumped right into him. At least that's how I saw it. But the ref saw it differently, or maybe he was still angry about Alex. Anyway, he called the foul on John, and the booing was so loud it matched the thunder outside.

Raible used his last time-out. "Get with it, Joe!" he shouted. "This is it! Everything we've worked for all year. We didn't come this far just to give up!"

Was that what I was doing? Was that why I'd worked myself to death in the morning, so that we'd lose the game and I wouldn't have to worry about having to pay off the devil? I looked at the faces of my teammates then — at the guys who were on the court and the guys on the bench. I thought about Snellinger, Doyle, and Reynolds in the locker room. I thought about all the practices and all the games. I thought about John in the summer, playing hard and steady, day after day. All that work going down the drain because I was dogging it, off in some dreamland of my own. It wasn't fair. I had to play, no matter what the consequences might be. There was no other way.

When we took the court, Stamets set a solid screen on the right side and Burns came around it perfectly. I hit him with a solid chest pass and he went up for the fifteen-footer. Swish! That bucket gave us a quick boost. If he had missed that one, we might not have come back no matter what I did. But when his hoop went down, we were in the game.

And Bellarmine let up, just a little. They saw four starters on the bench and they figured they had us. They were a little soft on defense and a little lazy on offense. Stamets and I ran a sweet pick-and-roll for a lay-in that cut their lead to five with two minutes left, and Maier knocked it down to three with a fifteen-foot bank shot twenty seconds later. When Rob Jenkins was fouled and sunk a pair of free throws, we were only down by one.

They tried to run some clock, and they did get it under a minute before Nielsen shuffled his feet and turned it over on a traveling violation.

I figured the guys would go to me, but Stamets worked the ball down into the corner to Burns. There were thirty-five seconds left — an eternity in a basketball game — but Burns lost his head and threw up a brick. It hit the front rim, and there were three Bellarmine players ready to gobble up the rebound. I don't know how he did it, and I'm sure the Bellarmine guys don't know either, but Jason Maier stuck his hand right in the middle of all of them and tipped it in. We were up by one and we were only twenty seconds from a perfect season!

Bellarmine inbounded. We immediately switched out of our zone and into a man-to-man defense to try to confuse them. Their point guard passed to the forward on the left side. Jenkins was in his face — tough defense and no foul. Back it went up top and then over to the right wing to my man. I could feel the defense dropping away behind me. They were clearing out the side. It was one-on-one basketball, him against me.

He gave me a little head fake, but I didn't bite. I knew he was going right. He wasn't strong with his left hand dribble, and this was crunch time. The instant he put the ball on the floor I slid over to block the baseline. He almost lost the ball out of bounds, and he almost charged into me. But I've got to give him credit. Somehow he pulled up, kept control, and even got a shot off. It was a fadeaway from about fourteen feet, an off-balance prayer. It hit the front rim, teetered there, and then dropped off. Jenkins was on the rebound like a hawk. He cleared it to me. I dribbled to half court, avoiding the Bellarmine players who were trying to foul me. I looked at the clock just as the horn sounded, and then I threw the ball way up into the rafters. We were 24–0! The championship was ours; the perfect season was ours; the berth in the state tournament was ours!

A second later, there was a ring of guys surrounding me. We high-fived and low-fived one another. We hugged, then we hugged again. We didn't walk off that court, we danced off.

When we hit the shower room, we started howling, and the noise echoed all through the room.

Stamets started drumming on his locker, and pretty soon everybody else was banging away at something. I was right in the middle of a full-throated, rock-concert shout when I felt a hand on my shoulder.

It was Raible.

"You'd better dress quickly, Joe. Your father has had another heart attack."

13

I didn't shower. I didn't really even change. I just pulled my street clothes over my uniform and hustled to the parking lot. Raible drove me to the hospital; my mother had already left.

It took thirty minutes, but it felt like we were in the car for hours. Raible had an old Plymouth that rattled over every bump. We didn't talk. My father was dead and I knew it. There was nothing to say. I watched the miles click away on the odometer. Those spinning digits numbed me. I decided that when I was in the funeral car, I'd watch those numbers. I'd watch them and nothing else. That was the only possible way to get through it.

Raible dropped me off at the emergency entrance. The woman at the information desk typed my father's name into the computer. "I don't show a Joseph Faust," she said. "If he was admitted, he didn't come through here."

For a second I was reassured. There must have been some mistake. My father was probably sitting on the sofa at home, wondering where I was. Then I realized that if he had died on the way to the hospital, they might not bring him to the emergency room.

I ran over to the main desk. Again a nurse typed his name into a computer. She misspelled it the first time, but when she tried again she calmly wrote the number "303" on a piece of paper and handed it to me.

The elevator was right around the corner. I pressed the button, but I couldn't wait, so I ran up the stairs. The instant I opened the door I saw my mother. She was crying. I hurried over to her and she hugged me.

"He's dead, isn't he?"

"No, he's all right," she whispered. "Whatever it was, it was minor. They're not even sure it was a heart attack."

We went into his room together. He didn't look pale and gray the way he had before. He looked fine. He had on his favorite red plaid bathrobe. He sat on the bed reading *Newsweek,* his glasses down on the tip of his nose.

"How was your game?" he asked.

"What?"

"Your basketball game."

"Oh, that. We won."

Then my mother stepped forward and they talked.

I don't know what they said. I didn't pay any attention. I stood off to the side for about five minutes, and then excused myself and walked down the hall until I found the men's room. I went into one of the stalls, closed the door, sat down on the toilet seat, and cried.

Late that night in bed I suddenly felt free. I didn't have to solve anything. My father was alive. The twenty-four games had been played. The devil's work — if he had done any — was over.

I didn't know what was going to happen next, but I knew one thing: for the first time in a long time, I was totally on my own. It was an incredible feeling.

PART
FIVE

1

At school Monday there was a pep rally before lunch. It was embarrassing. They had us sit on folding chairs in the middle of the gym while hundreds of kids spelled out the name of the school, letter by letter. Mr. Rowe congratulated Coach Raible, and Coach Raible thanked Mr. Aguirre, the athletic director. Then Raible addressed the students.

"This team has worked hard," he said, "and we've come a long way. But we wouldn't have made it without your support. And we're going to need your support this weekend. Together, we can go the distance!"

The student body cheered. After that, in the hallways some of the guys patted me on the back and some girls did, too. "Good luck!" I kept hearing those words over and over.

I was afraid I'd need it. All Monday I kept

wondering if I'd step on the court and be back where I was at the beginning of the year — missing shots, losing rebounds, having the ball go right through my hands. I'd been terrible, but at least all that had taken place during gym class. Next game I'd be playing in front of thousands of people.

I wanted to scrimmage at practice so I could find out right away if I'd lost anything. But everybody else was tired, physically and emotionally. Raible saw it, and he had the sense to back off. We just walked through our plays and then worked on our defensive sets. It wasn't what I wanted, but it was the right thing to do. You can't stay up forever, and there's always a danger of peaking too soon and leaving your game at practice. Besides, we were banged up, though it wasn't as bad as it could have been.

Snellinger's ankle sprain was minor. He'd be able to play again by Thursday at the latest. Doyle's teeth were OK, too. "I knew I didn't have to come out," he said. "I think that doctor was the father of one of the Bellarmine guys."

Practice ended with a little three-on-two fast-break drill, and then a rebounding game where you keep the ball alive off the backboard. After we'd gone through the line five times, Raible blew his whistle.

"You guys can shoot around," he said, "or you can go home. It's up to you."

Most of the guys went straight for the shower, but not John.

"How about a little horse, Joe?" he said.

We talked through the whole game, and I didn't even keep particularly close tabs on how many letters I had, or John had, or any of that. But when John knocked down a jumper from the free-throw line, he told me I had to make it or lose.

"No sweat," I said, but my shot was flat. It hit the back of the rim and bounded out.

We played again and I lost. "One more," I said, and even though I didn't laugh or joke around at all, nothing changed. I had *s*, and John tried a sweeping hook from the corner.

"Nasty!" he shouted when it tickled the twine.

I threw up an air ball to seal my third loss in a row. "That's enough," I said. "You're too good for me today."

"You're losing your touch," he joked as we headed to the shower.

When I opened the front door that evening, my father was sitting with my mother on the sofa looking at old photographs.

He smiled at me. "Cardialgia," he said. "That's a fancy name for heartburn. I feel like an idiot."

I went over and gave him a hug. I didn't think about it — if I had I'm sure I wouldn't have done it — it just happened. "I'm glad you're home, Dad."

"Glad to be home."

When I let go of him, he told me the doctor said he could go to the games. "Apparently sitting at home secreting large amounts of stomach acid is worse for me than going to the Coliseum and screaming my lungs out. What do you think of that?"

The three of us spent the rest of the evening flipping through old photograph albums. On one page we came across a picture of me on my fourth birthday. I had on a party hat and I was tottering, arms outstretched, toward our black cat, Midnight.

"Remember that day?" my mother asked.

"Sure," I said.

"Whatever happened to Midnight?" my father asked.

"Don't you remember?" my mother said. "He ran away one Fourth of July and never came back."

"He probably found a new home," my father said.

I shook my head. "He probably got hit by a car."

2

John had been joking about my shooting slump, but I wasn't laughing on Tuesday. I had lost the feel for the ball.

The strange thing is, I knew what I was doing wrong: I wasn't following through. When you shoot, you flick your wrist forward and your fingers end up pointing right at the hoop. I was jerking my hand back the instant I let the ball go. I lost the good arc, the nice backspin.

It's not that I missed everything. I still hit my lay-ins, of course, and from twelve feet and under I could use the glass and bank a decent percentage home. But even when a shot went in, it didn't feel right — it didn't feel like my shot.

I went to the free-throw line after practice on Tuesday to try to work through it. I bent my knees, I made sure I had plenty of loft, and I flicked my fingers forward. There were times when I thought I had the slump beat. I'd sink four or five free throws in a row, and then take the ball off the line and try to put down a few running jumpers. But the feel didn't come back. I'd start thinking about all the parts of my shot, and once I did that I was through. You can't think about form and shoot at the same time. That's being mechanical, and machines don't have any touch.

I tried to tell myself that my slump was just one of those things and that I'd come out of it, but I kept seeing myself going zero for fifteen in front of fourteen thousand people.

The night after Wednesday's practice I tried to convince my mother that my father should stay home. "Why risk it?" I said. "There's no point. It's just a basketball game." I kept imagining him gasping out his life in the bleachers while I was tossing up air balls on the court.

But my mother would have none of it. "I don't understand you," she snapped. "For years you complained that your father wouldn't go to your games. Now it's the biggest game of your life. He wants to go, the doctor says he can go, and you're putting up roadblocks and smoke screens to keep him away. Well, he is going, and I am going, and that is final."

On Thursday we scrimmaged. Raible had the second string play a full-court zone press — vintage UCLA. "That's what got Richland here, and that's what we've got to beat if we're going to advance."

I broke the press without much trouble. But I knew it didn't mean anything. Our second string had no experience clamping a zone press on. Richland's first string had been using one for twenty-five games.

My passing was sharp, and so was my defense, but I couldn't buy a basket in that scrimmage. It reached the point where Burns backed off me, daring me to take the shot. With him sagging low, the passing lanes were clogged and our whole offense sputtered. I had no choice. I shot over the top — and I missed. Time after time I missed. For once I was glad when Raible blew the whistle ending practice.

I didn't go in, though. I ran down a basketball and drifted over to a side hoop to work on my shot. I'd put up a couple of jumpers when John came over.

"Give it a rest, Joe," he said. "Your shot will be

there when you need it. There's such a thing as too much practice, you know."

He was right. I took a deep breath, put the ball back on the rack, and headed to the locker room with him.

"We're going to win," he said as he picked up a couple of towels. "I know you don't believe it, but we are."

3

It was stormy on Friday, but you could tell spring was near. Dark clouds swirled overhead. Then the sun would shoot out from behind them, only to disappear again. Once the sky was a mass of gray to the west, while to the east it was blue. Sometimes the wind would come up. I could see the trees swaying outside Monbouquette's window, and I could hear the branches rubbing against the window.

When I got home that afternoon, I sat in my room and stared at the clock. If I could have, I think I might have locked the door, turned off the light, and stayed in bed until the tournament was over.

But my parents were downstairs pacing around nervously. "It's four o'clock," my father yelled up at me. "Time to go."

I stuffed my jockstrap, two pairs of socks, my basketball shoes, and my uniform into my Adidas bag. Then I closed the door and went downstairs.

There were eight teams in the tournament. Loyal High was the big favorite. Even though we were the only other unbeaten team, nobody thought we had a real chance. We'd only played two good teams all year, the newspaper said. We couldn't possibly stand up to three tough games in three nights.

Being the underdog was a relief. If we lost, if I played like a scrub, at least it wouldn't be headlines. The other teams were going to get the ink.

I was glad about another thing, too. Our game was first. Tip-off was at five o'clock. Most people would come for the later games, so at least I wouldn't humiliate myself in front of a packed house.

In the locker room before the game Raible wanted us to say a prayer, so we all bowed our heads while he murmured something none of us could hear. After that the locker room went dead quiet. We were all too scared to talk.

The door suddenly swung open. "You take the court in five minutes, Coach," a voice yelled. The door closed.

I sat on the floor and stretched, bending forward until my nose touched my knees, and holding the stretch for a twenty count. I relaxed, then did it again. Next I did the hurdler's stretch, and finally, the butterfly. As my muscles loosened, I gave myself a little pep talk. "You're a player. You've always been a player. Relax. Everything will be fine."

I expected the Coliseum to be empty, but not as

empty as it was. Our school was out in force, and so was Richland, but the students were seated so far away it didn't feel like anyone was cheering. The section right behind the basket was deserted. As we shot around, I couldn't believe what a difference that made. Everything I threw up was short. The sound of the ball was wrong. It thudded dully like it was flat. And the place was cold, I guess because there were ten thousand empty seats. I was used to small, sweaty gyms. This was the biggest game of the year and the atmosphere was zero.

But when the horn sounded, everything changed. I checked in at the scorer's table and spotted Coach Bonner two rows up. He gave me a wink and a thumbs-up. I couldn't be sure, but I thought the man next to him was probably Eastern Washington's head coach. My knees went to Jell-O, and when I yelled, "Let's do it!" my voice sounded like I was near tears.

Richland is right near the Hanford nuclear power reservation. Their nickname is the Bombers. I never did find out if that was some sort of joke, but it fit their basketball team. The word was that their guards fired up three-pointers and their forwards and center crashed the boards.

I had a strong feeling I'd learn my fate right away, and I was right. They controlled the tip but missed their first shot. John rebounded and hit me with a great outlet pass. I gave a little stutter-step dribble and blew right past the last guy who could have stopped me. Suddenly I was free in the open court, streaking to the basket.

I went up, the ball over my head, flying in for a thunderous slam-dunk that would shake the rafters and rip through the net. And as I went up I knew that slam-dunk would shake off all the doubts that had been growing all season. That dunk was going to free me.

But instead of hitting nothing but net, I caught all iron, jamming the ball against the front of the rim. The force knocked me flat on my back, and I remember hearing my head hit the floor. Then everything went black. When I opened my eyes again, all the guys were peering down at me.

"Are you all right?" John asked.

I tried to stand up, but a little bald man told me to lay still.

"There's a stretcher coming," he said.

In the locker room I wanted to lie down, but the little man wouldn't let me. He stuck smelling salts under my nose, put an ice pack on my head, and started drilling me with questions. "What is your name? . . . What day is it? . . . How many fingers am I holding up?"

I answered him, but my voice sounded funny and my head ached. I wished he would just leave me alone. All I wanted to do was sleep.

He pulled up a chair in the runway and made me

watch the game. I couldn't see much of anything. I don't how know long I sat there before remembering I was supposed to be playing. I started up. "I've got to get back out there. What am I doing in here?"

I tried to stand, but the little man stopped me. "You are done for today, Tiger. If you sit still and keep wide awake, I'll let you stay here. Otherwise, it's to the hospital with you right now."

I sat back down. So this is how it ends, I thought. One stupid, showboat play and it's over.

From where we were, neither of us could even see the court. The little man would run out for a few minutes, and then run back and tell me the score.

"Twenty-two to nineteen, Richland. There's one minute until halftime."

Cold water dripped down my back, but he wouldn't get me fresh ice. "It'll keep you awake. That's the important thing."

I may have been awake, but I sure wasn't alert. I vaguely heard the bands playing and then the horn for the second half. After that I just remember him running back and forth shouting numbers at me, and I remember my head throbbing. The numbers were always close, and that surprised me.

"Fifty-six to fifty-six! Richland's got the ball and there are only eighteen seconds left."

I came out of the fog, then. I wanted to be out there. Even though I was sure we'd lose, I wanted to be on the court. I didn't want to be in any stupid side aisle with some little old man; I wanted to be with the guys.

The little man ran up the aisle. I heard screaming and then a great gasp, then more screaming and the horn. The band started playing and the little man was standing over me shouting, "You've won! You've won! Eastside's won!"

The instant the game was over, my parents were in the locker room. My father was furious.

"Why were we kept out of here?" he demanded.

The little man shrugged. "I don't know. There must have been some mistake. Who kept you out?"

My father pointed toward the court. "The security guard kept us out, that's who!"

The little man looked in the direction my father had indicated. There were probably one hundred people milling about, at least ten of them in some uniform or another.

"Which guard?"

"Forget it," he snapped. "I'm taking my son to the hospital for an X ray, if that's permissible."

"Yes, certainly. That is a good precaution. I recommend that."

4

We drove straight to the emergency room of University Hospital. I was still a little woozy, and when a guy came in with his chopped-off finger stuck in a bag of ice, I almost passed out.

"Nothing serious," the doctor said when the X ray came back. "Just a bad bump. Take it easy for a week or two."

He'd almost disappeared back into the emergency room when his words sunk in. "A week!" I hollered. "I can't wait a week. I've got a game tomorrow."

After the doctor heard me out, he backed down a bit. "All right," he said. "If your team makes the finals, and if you don't have any headaches, then you can play on Sunday. But you absolutely cannot play tomorrow. Understand?"

Once we got home that night I went upstairs and turned on the radio to get the scores of the other games. The sportscaster mentioned us, of course, and Shadle Park and Foss, the other winners in the first round. But the spotlight was on Loyal High. The reporter called them "the clear favorite, the class of the tournament." Then he went on to say that Ross was "the best player this state has seen in years." It made me sick, so I switched off the radio.

Everything was a mystery to me — most of all myself. Five hours earlier I hadn't wanted to take the court. Now I had the perfect excuse to stay out of the games, and more than anything I wanted to play.

I tried to be logical. I went to my desk, took out a piece of paper, and wrote down all the reasons I was sure I'd sold my soul to the devil. Then I wrote down all the reasons why I couldn't possibly have sold my soul. The two sides balanced. I crumpled up the paper and threw it in the trash.

I picked my basketball up off the floor, lay down on my bed, and started it spinning on my fingertip. I swatted the side of the ball to make it spin even faster, and then I swatted it again. Pretty soon I forgot all about the devil and just concentrated on keeping that basketball spinning on my fingertip. I got it going faster that night than I ever had before. And I didn't even have to move my elbow much to keep it balanced. It was like the ball was attached to my finger, like it was part of me.

5

The next thing I knew it was noon. I hadn't set my alarm and no one had awakened me. We had a shoot-around at twelve-thirty. Even though I couldn't play, I wanted to be there.

I ran downstairs. By the time I reached the bottom step my head throbbed. No one was home. I was furious. How could my parents have left me alone like that? Then I saw a note on the kitchen table.

I let you sleep because you needed it. I called
Mr. Raible and explained. Take it easy. We'll
be back by 4:00.

Love, Mom

I scrambled some eggs and tried to watch TV. I
couldn't follow the game shows and the sitcoms
were just too stupid. I gave the remote a workout
for at least thirty minutes before I quit. There was
nothing to do but wait.

Our game was at seven. By six I was in the locker
room in a coat and tie. The guys all shook my hand
and told me what a tough break it was. I ached to
play; sitting at the end of the bench in hard shoes
was not the way I wanted to go out.

The first quarter was awful. The guys were tight.
John threw up an air ball from eight feet, Ray traveled twice, and Stamets just plain wouldn't shoot.
Shadle Park was playing a straight up man-to-man,
and I knew how I would attack it. But I wasn't
playing. I felt like screaming — it was so frustrating
to have to sit and watch. We were supposed to be
two of the best four teams in the state, but it was
only 11–8, Shadle Park, at the quarter.

Raible rested Eddie at the opening of the second
quarter. Eddie came to the end of the bench, sucked
down some Gatorade, and then sank into the folding chair next to me, his head between his knees.

"Do you see anything, Joe?" he asked, once he'd
caught his breath.

"What?"

"That I can do differently. Do you see anything?"

I couldn't play, but I could talk. The words came rushing out of me. I told him that Ray had a mismatch, that the clear-out would work for Alex, that John was overmatched inside and wasn't going to score much, and that he had to make Stamets shoot.

"Take charge," I said. "Let them know you're running things, and act like you know what you're doing — even if you don't!"

In a movie, Eddie would have gone out there and everything would have changed instantly. It didn't happen like that. As a matter of fact, the first time he touched the ball he turned it over. But on the next trip he ran the clear-out for Alex and it worked as it had in practice. After that, the guys slowly loosened up. Ray stuck back a couple of offensive rebounds. Eddie made a nice steal and hit a driving lay-up. Stamets popped in a three-pointer from the top of the key.

I sat in my street clothes at the end of the bench and watched the team turn itself around. I could hardly believe what I saw. Doyle hadn't played the point in weeks, so there was a little miscommunication, but even so the team was *good*. I always knew John could play, but I hadn't noticed all the little things the other guys did. Snellinger set solid screens, Stamets scrapped for every loose ball, Reynolds denied his man position, over and over.

And I watched another thing, too. I watched the

second-stringers cheer. Not one of them was going to see more than a few minutes of action and they knew it. Yet they had given everything they had at every practice. They had pushed the first team, they had pushed us to be better. They weren't on the court, but their sweat was in the game.

As we pulled away from Shadle Park and took that final step into the championship game, I felt ashamed. I'd been so wrapped up in myself that I'd been blind to the team. I'd believed that without me they couldn't win, that they were nothing. But it was the other way around.

In the locker room after the victory the guys went crazy. They hugged and shouted and cheered. Standing there in my coat and tie, I felt out of it. I tried to slip out the door.

John spotted me. "Joe," he shouted, "where are you going?"

"Home."

"No, you're not. Raible's taking us all out to Chicago's for pizza. Tell your parents I can take you home." He came over to me, put his arm around my shoulder, and gave me a good shake. "Can you believe it, Joe? We won both these games without you. Think what will happen tomorrow night when you're playing again."

6

In the Sunday paper I read all about our astonishing upset and about Loyal High's destruction of Foss. The stage was set for the championship game: two Seattle-area schools, both undefeated, one private, the other public. For the first time ever, ticket scalpers were making money on a high-school game.

I moped around the house all morning and most of the afternoon. I felt like I had to go somewhere, like I had to do something, but I couldn't think where or what. Then, at four o'clock it hit me.

I ran all the way. It was four-thirty by the time I reached it, and the light was fading. It had begun to drizzle, but I didn't care. The boards I'd pulled back months earlier were still off, so I snuck in just as I had before.

Nothing had changed. The light was playing the same strange tricks. There was the real hoop in front of me. Its fantastic, shadowy double flickered on the wall behind it. I bounced the ball and heard the dull thud followed by an eerie echo.

The drizzle turned to a hard rain. I could hear it pound on the sheet-metal roof. My heart was pounding, too.

I went to the exact spot where I had swished ten in a row. I eyed the hoop, took a deep breath, and buried the first shot. I picked up the ball, moved it to my fingertips, bent my knees, jumped, and released: Swish! Three, four, five in a row. Once again my rhythm was so perfect that the backspin brought the ball right back to me. Six in a row! Seven . . .

At that moment I stopped and looked around. I was standing in an old gym. It was dirty, dark, and poorly lit, but it was just an old gym, and I was just shooting baskets. Nothing more, nothing less. I had sunk seven in a row — seven perfect swishes. What would it prove if I made, or didn't make, three more? What would it have proved if I'd missed on my second try? Or my fifth? I'd never know for sure what had happened on November 16, never.

I didn't take any more shots. Instead, I swooped in for a final lay-in and then put the ball under my arm and left the old gym for the final time. I had a game to play in a few hours; I couldn't waste my energy.

Just as I poked my head out the hole, a police car came around the corner. It stopped and I felt the heat of a spotlight on my face. For a second I thought about hiding, so I ducked my head back inside. But then I crawled out and stood up.

The policemen got out of their car and came up to me. One of them shone his flashlight right in my face. The other one asked me what I was doing.

"I wanted to shoot baskets," I answered. "It started to rain and I knew there was a gym in there. I saw the hole, so I climbed in."

"Don't I know you?" the cop with the flashlight asked. "What's your name?"

"Joe Faust."

"Joe Faust!" he said excitedly. He nudged his partner. "This kid is the star of Eastside's basketball team."

His partner grunted.

"Look, Faust," the first cop said, "you don't want to get run in for breaking and entering on the day of the championship game, do you?"

"No, sir."

"Then you take your basketball and move it. And don't let me catch you around here again."

I didn't wait for a second invitation. I walked away fast, but not so fast that they'd think I was running.

7

When I reached home, my mother had a small dinner waiting: chicken sandwiches and celery sticks. Ever since my father's heart attack we were eating nothing but fish, skinless chicken, and mounds of vegetables. I didn't like it much. Still, if my father had to eat rabbit food to stay alive, then I'd eat it too.

We chatted all through the meal. Nervous talk — no one mentioned the game. As we were finishing, my father finally brought it up. "It'd go easier on my heart if you won big." We all laughed, but that kind of talk made me nervous, and I could tell my mother didn't think it was much of a joke, either.

"We'll blow them out," I promised.

We left the house at six-thirty. I must have checked to see that I had my gear ten times. When we were three miles from home, I was certain I'd forgotten my jockstrap. I rifled through my bag and found two of them at the bottom.

I half expected an accident, or a massive traffic jam, or a flat tire, or something to make us late. But at seven they dropped me off outside the players' entrance. My father looked like he wanted to say something, but the guy behind him honked and he had to drive off.

I stood alone in the dark outside the Coliseum. It was a huge building, gray and quiet. I felt small next to it. There were rain puddles on the pathway to the players' gate.

I showed my pass to an old lady at the door. She nodded. "Good luck, Sonny." I walked in and peeked onto the court. Shadle Park was playing Foss in the consolation game. The Coliseum was about half full, but most of the people were milling around. It was our game they'd come to see.

I stood outside the locker room for a moment before going in. There were no more magic spells to save me. I was on my own. When I opened the door, I saw Eddie and Ray sitting on the wooden bench. Ray looked ghostly. "I've been barfing for the past hour," he said.

One by one the rest of the guys filtered in.

Occasionally someone would come in full of phony go-go spirit, but the general terror was infectious.

Raible called us together before we took the court. "Play loose," he advised. He was so tight he could hardly speak. "Take your shots when you're open. It's been a great year. Let's make it unbelievable."

We let out a weak cheer and ran onto the court. The bands played and the cheerleaders cheered, and suddenly it felt like just another game. The court was the same size, the ball was the same, the number of players was the same. It was a basketball game, and basketball is a sport I play well. I took a deep breath, and when I exhaled my nervousness went out. I was ready to play.

8

The horn sounded and we hustled over to the bench. The light dimmed and then, one by one, we were introduced, a spotlight picking us out as we ran to center court. We gave each other exaggerated high-fives as the applause swept over us.

Then Loyal High was introduced. They high-fived each other just as we had. When Ross's name was called, the decibel level went up and he broke into a wide grin.

The whistle blew and the starters took the court. The ref tossed the ball up. After a scramble, I snatched it near mid-court and slowly dribbled it up. The long wait was over: the game was on.

I took the ball down into the corner. Immediately, Loyal High double-teamed. I panicked, spun around, and launched a wild twenty-footer. It hit nothing. The Loyal High rooters chanted: "Air ball, air ball!"

As I backpedaled on defense, I told myself to calm down, to lead the team and not worry about leading in scoring. If they were going to double-team me, then I was going to pass off.

Ross took an entry pass at the high post, spun into the key, and sank a jumper. I took the inbounds pass and went right back down to the corner. Again they double-teamed. This time I spotted the open man: Ray had broken to the hoop and I hit him with a crisp bounce pass for an easy bucket.

The huge crowd was oddly quiet that first half. They kept waiting for Loyal High to blow us right out of the gym. It never happened, though Ross was almost unstoppable. He was hitting one sensational shot after another: spinning jumpers, driving hooks, reverse lay-ins. But no one else on Loyal High's team had gotten untracked, and we were getting our baskets, too. Every once in a while they'd come with that double-team trap, and most of the time I'd make them pay.

Though the explosion everyone expected didn't happen, there was an explosion. The score was

32–30 with one minute left before halftime when it happened. Ross missed a close-in jumper. John snatched the rebound and whipped a quick outlet pass to me. Eddie had snuck behind the defense, and I hit him right in the hands with a pass that should have resulted in a tying basket. But out of nowhere Loyal High's big forward, Danny Melton, came flying across the court. He didn't have a prayer of blocking the shot, so he clotheslined Doyle and sent him crashing into the basket support. Eddie went down and stayed down. Melton popped right back up and walked away. He didn't even look to see how badly Eddie was hurt. He just strutted away, almost smirking.

I think it was the smirk that enraged John. He raced the length of the court, ready to punch it out with Melton. Ross saw what John was going to do and tackled him. As those two grappled on the ground, Melton stood above them with his fists clenched. Both benches emptied. Pushing and shoving matches broke out all over the court. Even Raible was out there, yelling at Loyal High's coach.

It took ten minutes to restore order. Doyle looked dazed and missed both free throws. We got the ball on the intentional foul but turned it over on a three-second violation. Loyal High ran the clock down to ten seconds and then Ross hit a jumper over John. We were down 34–30 when the horn sounded ending the first half.

9

In the locker room nobody talked basketball. All the talk was of revenge. "We can't let them get away with that stuff," Raible bellowed. "They might beat us, but I'll be damned if they are going to push us around!" The anger was infectious, and I caught it too.

That third quarter was more of a hockey game than it was a basketball game. Elbows were flying on the rebounds and every other screen was accompanied by a forearm shot. The refs let too much of the dirty stuff go.

Tempers were hot; our play was ice-cold. We were all looking at one another instead of moving. Loyal High kept up the double-team trap, but in that third quarter none of the guys cut to the hoop, or if they did, I didn't see them. I tossed up five desperation jumpers that quarter, and if I hadn't gotten two good rolls, I would have come up empty.

Luckily, Loyal High was as caught up in the bruise battle as we were. Ross scored on a great driving lay-in just before the end of the quarter. Even so, they were only up by six.

During the break between quarters Raible kept the fires burning. "Don't back off. Show these guys what you're made of. The whole state is watching."

But what were they watching? That's the question I asked myself as we headed back onto the court for the start of the fourth quarter. It certainly wasn't good basketball.

And it didn't improve; it just got rougher. Neither team could get any momentum going because the game had no flow. The season drained away minute by minute. Loyal High kept the lead around five or six, and we just couldn't cut into it.

There were less than four minutes left when Melton caught John with a vicious elbow to the Adam's apple. The refs didn't see it, or didn't call it, and John was gasping for breath on his knees at one end of the court while Ross was hitting a jumper at the other end.

Our fans saw the elbow, though, and even on the court I could tell that the mood in the stands had turned ugly. Both the boos and the cheers grew louder and louder and were punctuated by obscene shouts from all around the Coliseum. I thought I saw a brawl in one of the upper balconies. It was as if we were all so many sticks of dynamite. The fuses had been burning down; it was just a question of time.

We scored, cutting the lead back to six. Then everything blew up.

Loyal High had the ball. Melton set a baseline screen. Ross cut to the hoop, and, as John followed, Melton moved his foot six inches and tripped him. It wasn't any dirtier than many of the plays in the game, but in an instant Ray had Melton in a headlock and was punching him in the face.

Again, both benches emptied. This time real fights broke out.

As soon as the fighting began, I spotted a purple jersey moving up toward me. I wheeled around, fists ready.

It was Ross. He had his hands up like a cowboy in a western. "Easy, Joe," he said. "We don't need this."

A part of me wanted to deck him. But I didn't swing.

We walked down under the hoop away from all the fighting. The crowd was roaring; blood was pouring from Melton's nose; the refs were red-faced from blowing their whistles and charging around the court.

Neither Ross nor I spoke. I don't know how he felt, but it seemed to me that we were in a charmed circle, in the eye of a hurricane.

It must have been at least fifteen minutes before the refs got everyone back to the benches. Snellinger was ejected. Melton staggered off to the trainer's room, probably with a broken nose. Both coaches were warned that if any player on either bench set foot on the court, he would be ejected and the other team would shoot a double technical.

As we huddled before going back onto the court, I looked in John's eyes, in Eddie's eyes, in Alex's, and Maier's. All I saw was fury. "Listen," I said, "this is the championship game and we've done everything but play basketball."

When we took the court, I went straight over to

Ross and shook his hand. After that I went to each of the Loyal High players and shook hands. I'm sure it looked like Goody Two-Shoes grandstanding, but I didn't care. Enough was enough.

John got the tip and Eddie fed me with a nice pass. I hit a ten-footer from the right side and we were down by four.

"Defense!" I shouted, and I could tell the team had finally clicked into basketball. We had our hands up and our eyes were on the ball.

Loyal High went into a weave. We let them run a few passes, and then we tightened the pressure. John tipped one pass and we almost got it. Then Alex slapped the ball out of his man's hands and pounced on it.

I brought the ball up quickly and took it deep into the corner. That drew the double-team, and I hit Alex, who banked home a six-footer. We were down by two.

I thought they might panic then and do something stupid. I should have known better. Loyal High didn't get to be 26–0 by folding under pressure. They coolly set up their offense. I wanted to deny the entry pass to Ross, but I couldn't do it. When they got it to him, he faked the spin move into the key. John figured Ross was going to put it up. He left his man, and Ross made him pay with a beautiful bounce pass for an easy backdoor lay-in. Loyal High by four again, with less than a minute left.

Eddie brought the ball up. Alex set a screen for me. I came around it, caught the ball, and in one motion went up for the shot. I felt a slap on the elbow, but I kept my eye on the hoop and released the ball just as the whistle blew. The shot hit the back of the rim and went in. When I sank the free throw, we were down by one, with twenty-two seconds left.

The crowd was on its feet. They roared and stomped through the entire time-out. Raible was shouting instructions about when to foul, but I couldn't hear.

We tried to keep Loyal High from getting the ball in, but Ross darted to center court and they hit him. He held the ball until Alex applied some pressure. Then he dribbled twice and passed off. Sixteen seconds left.

They went into the four-corners. We were up in their faces, but we couldn't force the turnover. Nine seconds left. Ross got the ball on the right side. I picked him up on the switch. He was looking for a cutter, and I was looking for a steal. Suddenly, Ross put the ball on the floor and broke by me toward the hoop. It was the last thing I thought he'd do, but somehow John was ready. He went up with Ross and blocked the lay-in cleanly. The ball rolled free for a moment, then Alex went to the floor to wrestle it away from everybody. I took off on the fast break as Alex hit Doyle at half court.

I remember hearing the crowd chant "Five! Four!

Three!" as the last seconds ticked away. After "Three!" everything went silent for me. I only remember what I saw.

Eddie heaved the ball toward the basket. I don't know whether it was a pass or a shot, and I never asked him. But as I raced toward the hoop I could see it was off-line. I was sure the ball was too far in front of me, that I'd never reach it, but still I went up, stretching, stretching like a wide receiver in football. I felt the ball at the very tips of my fingers, and then I looked for the hoop. Amazingly, it was there, rushing at me — but too close! I was sure I'd jam the ball against the front of the rim again. But from somewhere I found the extra spring. I went higher and higher, and the miracle happened. I slam-dunked it down and through.

The horn sounded. 64–63 Eastside. We were the champions!

The next thing I knew the court was alive with jumping, joyous fans. Ross shook my hand and disappeared with the other Loyal High players into the locker room. I looked up in the bleachers for my mother and father, but their seats were empty. Raible hugged me; John picked me up off the ground. I was swirled around so much my head was spinning. Then I saw my father. The police had formed a ring to keep the fans off the court. My father had shoved his way through the crowd, and actually had one foot on the hardwood floor. A policeman was trying to push him back, but he didn't seem to notice. He was just smiling and clapping. I wanted to go over to him, but I was swept into the locker room instead. All I could do was give him a little wave. He nodded and waved back.

10

We stayed in the locker room for about an hour. Raible had bought a case of sparkling apple cider, and we shook up the bottles, spraying one another. It was stupid, in a way, pretending we were the Lakers celebrating an NBA title. But it was the closest any of us were ever going to get, and besides, it was fun and none of us wanted to go home.

Then the janitors came in and blinked the lights. I dressed and met my parents outside the E Gate. We went to Pacific Desserts, where I ordered a piece of chocolate cake I couldn't eat. I talked nonstop about the game. By the time we reached home, we were all exhausted.

I filled the tub with hot water, and soaked. That's probably why I fell asleep once I got to bed, and I think I would have slept until morning if my stomach hadn't started rumbling around one-thirty. I woke up hungrier than I'd ever been in my life.

I slipped down into the kitchen, turned on the light over the stove, and silently made myself a peanut butter sandwich. I ate it, drank a glass of milk, and had started making another one when my father opened the door.

"I didn't wake you, did I?" I whispered.

"No," he said as he took down his Grape-Nuts from above the refrigerator. "I just thought I'd have a little snack."

We sat across from each other and ate in silence. The peanut butter tasted wonderful and the milk was ice-cold. When I looked out the window, I could see the limbs of the birch trees in our front yard, and I could also see our reflections in the glass.

"How's your head?" my father asked.

"Fine."

"No headache?"

"Nope."

After that we were silent for a few more moments, as if the stillness of the night had cast a spell over us.

"While you were celebrating in the locker room, Coach Bonner came over. We had quite a long talk about you. Do you know what he asked me?"

I felt my ears burning and my face go red.

"He asked me if I taught you how to play basketball. He said you play smart, like a coach's son."

I carried my plate to the sink, trying to work up my courage. "Dad," I said when I sat down again, "I've been meaning to talk to you about — "

"I know, Joe," my father interrupted. "Your mother told me. You want to go to Eastern Washington next year. You want to play basketball."

I nodded.

He looked out the window into the darkness. "When I was your age, my passion was science. All my life I've wanted it to be your passion, too. But it isn't, is it?"

"Not exactly."

My father smiled. "The funny thing is, my father wanted me to be an architect. He was a construction worker and he hated most of the projects he worked on. He said there was no excuse for an ugly building. He did his damnedest to force me into architecture." My father shook his head. "I would have made a lousy architect."

"And I'd make a lousy scientist."

My father sat straight up in the chair. "Oh, I don't think that's true. I think you could be a — " Then he caught himself, and stopped. "I'd better go up to bed now. And you'd better go to bed, too. Five more minutes and we'll be arguing."

I went upstairs, but I couldn't sleep. I kept thinking about playing college basketball, and I kept trying to believe it really could happen.

Finally I got out of bed and went over to the window. The sky was clear and the light from the full moon filled my room. Ever since third grade I'd been taught that it's not the moon's light at all, that it's light from the sun that reflects off the moon. Nothing new, but that night it seemed miraculous. Out there in space was a burning sun. Its light had traveled millions of miles, bounced off the moon, and come into my room. Wonderful things are happening all the time.

Epilogue

It's either the Buddhists or the Hindus who believe that everything repeats itself. There might be something to it. Two days after we won the championship, my father mailed my newspaper clippings to Stanford's coach and asked about my chances of making the team as a walk-on.

At first it made me mad, but then I thought, "Why not?" Pac-Ten ball would be an even bigger challenge than the Big Sky conference.

The coach wrote that if I was admitted to Stanford, I was welcome to try out. My father went crazy for two days. Then my SAT score came — eleven hundred. Good enough for Eastern Washington, but not good enough for Stanford.

The next morning my father started talking about calling the Dean of Admissions to see if he could use his influence to get me accepted anyway. Then we finally did have an argument, though not much of one. I said I didn't want any special treatment. He said I was being stubborn, that all he wanted to do was to open the door for me. I said I understood and that I appreciated the help he was trying to give me. But I also told him that from now on I'm only going through doors I open for myself.